The Insomniac Society

GABRIELLE LEVY

The Insomniac Society

Translated by Maren Baudet-Lackner

HODDER

First published in France in 2019 by JC Lattes
An Hachette France company

First published in Great Britain in 2021 by Hodder & Stoughton
An Hachette UK company

This paperback edition published in 2021

I

A CIP catalogue record for this title is available from the British Library

Paperback ISBN 978 1 529 32756 4
eBook ISBN 978 1 529 32715 1

Typeset in Plantin Light by Palimpsest Book Production Limited, Falkirk, Stirlingshire

Printed and bound in Great Britain by Clays Ltd, Elcograf S.p.A.

Hodder & Stoughton policy is to use papers that are natural, renewable
and recyclable products and made from wood grown in sustainable forests.
The logging and manufacturing processes are expected to conform to
the environmental regulations of the country of origin.

Hodder & Stoughton Ltd
Carmelite House
50 Victoria Embankment
London EC4Y 0DZ

www.hodder.co.uk

2 a.m. The bed is as soft as earth and with every turn of my tense, heavy body, I sink a little deeper. It's damp and cold. The room is pitch-black. I bury myself beneath the dust and everything turns to darkness. Every night I vanish from the surface of the earth, spiralling down in thoughts I can't control.

1

Monday, 8.10 a.m. I'm late. And the giant, slug-like mass of people crawling towards the Métro exit in front of me isn't helping. I thread my way through the ill-tempered crowd, eager to reach daylight as quickly as possible. Outside, the day is overcast. The clouds are low in the sky and the street is packed with scurrying people, their heads bowed against the cold.

I'm wearing a jumper that's far too thick for the early autumn weather, and as I battle sweatily through the throng, the stress begins to get to me. I missed the first session deliberately, but if I don't make it to this one, I'll never work up the courage to go at all. Stuck in this mad morning rush, I begin to wonder whether it's the days or the nights that are hardest for me. It's a close-run thing.

After an hour on the train and twenty minutes in the Métro, I'm half an hour late by the time I reach my destination: a modern building that matches the one I checked out on Google Maps. I spend another five minutes or so scanning the information board in the lobby to find the right floor. Then, three flights of stairs later, I finally enter the designated room – flushed, out of breath, and dripping with sweat, all hopes of looking even vaguely presentable dashed by the morning's efforts. Hoping to go unnoticed, I make for one of the many empty chairs and am about to sit down when I catch a waft of disinfectant, and instantly feel sick. The cold glare of the neon lights, the beige linoleum, and the slowly rising sun behind the window remind me of those early morning lessons at school, when it always felt like such a struggle to stay awake.

I study my fellow-sufferers warily. There are two of them. Only two – and both are female. One, wearing a sweater dress that's cinched at the waist with a thick braided belt, exudes a timeless elegance I can only dream of. It's hard to tell how old she is. Her misty grey hair is pulled up into a bun and her skin is marked by wrinkles, but her unusually bright eyes convey pure, child-like joy. I don't see any signs of fatigue in that radiant face.

The other woman couldn't be more different. Young and thin with dark hair dyed blonde framing a face that's as white as the neon lights, she looks at the end of her tether. Her cheeks are hollow and the circles under her eyes are enormous.

This is hopeless, I think to myself. I was expecting a full room where I would be able to make myself inconspicuous in the back row. You can't hide in a room where there are only three people sitting around a table.

A woman with greying hair – the person organising the course, I assume – is painstakingly drawing something on the whiteboard. Short and rather plump, she is conservatively dressed in black. When she's finished her diagram, she turns round, puts down her marker, and addresses me.

'I'm Hélène, a sleep psychologist. I'll be running the meetings,' she explains. 'You must be Claire?' Her tone is polite rather than warm.

Mine, despite my best efforts, is tense. 'I thought there would be more of us,' I say lamely.

'There should be five of you if all goes to plan. But let me introduce Michèle and Lena to start with.'

The younger of the two, Lena, offers me a limp wave, but Michèle flashes me a warm, welcoming smile that instantly puts me at my ease.

Hélène praises me for coming and assures me I will see results. I force a smile. I wish I could believe her, but, unfortunately, I'm pretty sceptical about this sort of thing. I'm only here because my husband went on and on at me to do something, and I finally gave in. Apparently, my insomnia has a negative impact on *his* sleep. As always, he had the last word and, as always, I let someone else make my decisions for me.

Five people if all goes to plan . . . I'm definitely not going to be able to go unnoticed.

Hélène picks up her marker again and goes over the content of the first session. The theme was, apparently, 'internal clocks'. Her voice gets louder as she warms to her subject – I can tell she takes it all very seriously.

'This lock, hidden away in our brains, sets our circadian rhythm – our night–day cycle. It regulates all our bodily processes – setting their tempo, if you will, like a miniature orchestra conductor!'

'I'll give you my notes,' whispers Michèle.

I wasn't expecting a lecture – I could have bought a book if that's what I wanted. Hélène turns to me again. 'Before you arrived, I was explaining the different sleep stages. I'll start again at the beginning. First, there's non-REM sleep, which is itself made up of three stages. Stage 1 is the transition between waking consciousness and sleep. In Stage 2 you're in a phase of light sleep where something like, say, a noise or bright light can wake you. When you reach Stage 3 you're completely cut off from the outside world. You're in a deep sleep, the most restorative form of sleep, and it's difficult to wake you. Next comes REM sleep, where your mind experiences intense brain activity with long, elaborate dreams, but your body . . .'

I stop listening. As far as I'm concerned, this Stage 3 deep sleep I've heard so much about is totally unattainable. A dream. Pie in the sky. A mirage in the desert. I am tempted to ask if insomniacs ever actually manage to achieve it, but a totally misplaced sense of pride holds me back. Michèle looks at me, then asks the question herself, as if she has somehow guessed what I have been thinking.

'It's a little complicated,' Hélène replies. 'Let's say that depression and other mood disorders can alter the structure of deep sleep. This anomaly leaves the patient feeling that their sleep is . . . disrupted. We'll have a chance to revisit this another time. Recent studies have identified other reasons that may explain why you can wake up feeling unrested. In any case, after falling asleep you're in a light sleep – Stages 1 and 2 – and then, after about twenty minutes, you find yourself in a deep sleep that lasts about . . .'

I'm losing focus. The wave of energy I felt as I walked in has evaporated in the heat of the room. I feel I am slipping back into that state between sleep and wakefulness that I know only too well. Lena takes a big spiral-bound notebook out of her backpack, which is torn to bits and held together by several safety pins. Her face disappears behind a curtain of hair. She starts taking notes. Michèle does the same, but first she tears out a few pages and hands them to me – unwittingly roping me in, whether I like it or not. I hadn't asked for any paper, but I accept it to be polite, and as she holds out her slim hand, I notice there are three bracelets on her wrist. They seem to be engraved with names, but I can't read them.

Hélène is still droning on about sleep stages when the piercing screams of a young child suddenly cut her off. Her features darken. I pull myself out of my torpor.

'Oh no, not again,' she sighs. 'I asked them to find us a new room for this session . . . I'm sorry, there's a dental surgery on the other side of the wall. This happens all the time.'

The screeching gets louder and louder for several minutes,

until a door slams and quick footsteps echo through the corridor. Silence. I make the most of the situation to suggest we find a space for our meetings that's quieter, more welcoming. We're talking about sleep, after all, not business matters. Michèle, her voice as cheerful as her eyes, suggests that perhaps things aren't as bad as we think, and offers to bring mugs, teabags and a thermos of hot water to make us feel more at home. As if hearing her for the first time, Lena marvels at how correctly she speaks.

'No doubt due to my profession, my dear Lena. I used to teach literature for university crammer courses.'

'Whenever I open my mouth my mum says I sound like a fishwife,' Lena says. She has drawn up one of her knees towards her chest and is chewing on a strand of hair. 'But who cares what room we're in? It's not like this is going to make any difference to our nights.'

'Shall we continue?' Hélène asks, slightly thrown by our having veered off-topic. 'As I was saying, a single cycle includes a short period of wakefulness, non-REM sleep, and REM sleep.'

She is about to begin drawing a new diagram when the door opens to reveal an anxious-looking face. A man, taller than average and somewhere between forty and fifty years of age, steps in and timidly asks if he's in the right place. 'I'm sorry to be late. I had some problems on the Métro. As for the first session, I went to the other centre – the one in the suburbs. You know, they have the same name . . . Sorry, I'm Hervé,' he says in a trembling voice. He has a disconcerting habit of nodding slightly as he speaks, which makes him look a bit odd.

Hélène ceremoniously crosses his name off the list and invites him to sit down.

He's thin as well as tall, which emphasises his height. His shoulders slump when he sits down, and he doesn't even bother to take off his trench coat or put down his leather briefcase, which he clutches tightly to his stomach. He reminds me of a shy new student that's turned up halfway through term.

Hélène asks him to introduce himself briefly, but no sooner does the spindly man open his mouth than the screams ring out again.

Hélène raises her voice so we can hear her. 'Our time is up anyway. Sorry, Hervé. We'll hear what you have to say next time. In two weeks. Make sure you write it down. The length of time between sessions will vary . . . Ah, I almost forgot . . . your sleep logs!'

'I must confess, I had a few problems filling mine out,' Michèle explains.

'Don't worry. We'll talk more about them next time. What about yours, Claire?'

'I haven't got it,' I reply dryly.

'Please try to bring it with you every time. It's the foundation of our work together. And the only way for us to get a clear picture of your nights. You'll be surprised at the difference it makes. I promise to find a better room for our next session. And don't forget: as long as you keep faith and don't give up hope, you can find your way back to sleep.'

I stifle a nervous chuckle. I feel as if I'm at an Alcoholics Anonymous meeting.

Lena stands up and hurries out of the room, muttering a quick goodbye over her shoulder and, for the first time, I notice how terribly skinny she is. I leave with Michèle and Hervé.

In the corridor we run into the hysterical child from next door. She's with her helpless-looking mother and is still screaming. Michèle stops in front of her, kneels down and whispers something in her ear, whereupon the little girl immediately stops howling and begins to study the strange person before her with apparent fascination. She then smiles and calmly walks back into the torture chamber, leaving her mother dumbfounded – and, I imagine, everlastingly grateful. Hervé and I watch in disbelief. Pleased with her efforts, Michèle stands up, adjusts her bun, and takes me by the arm as if we were old friends.

'Children aren't as difficult as we think,' she explains matter-of-factly.

As we wait silently for the lift, which seems to be taking forever to arrive, Hervé clears his throat, pushes his glasses up the bridge of his nose, and declares, 'I've been an insomniac for twenty years. And you?'

Tuesday, 12.30 a.m. Michèle walks quickly to warm herself up against the cold. She's watchful – wary even, although she's taken the same route at the same time every night for years. The little church sits between two blocks of flats. Easy to miss in broad daylight, it is barely noticeable in the dark. Michèle walks past it without slowing down, then takes an alleyway down the side of the church. At the foot of a stairwell leading to the side entrance, she lifts a small stone to find the key.

Despite the darkness, she moves around confidently, as if she were in her own home. She takes off her coat and disappears into a closet, where she fiddles with the fuse box until a dim light fills the space. She grabs a bucketful of soapy water and a mop and, wearing a light blue smock that's clearly not hers, makes her way towards the nave. Before getting down to work she takes a few coins out of her pocket and lights three candles. Then, hands tightly gripping the wooden mop handle, and shoulders hunched with a sense of purpose, she sets to with gusto. *Come on, children, finish your tea. Antoine, didn't you eat anything at the canteen? Stop bickering. How was school today? Don't worry, Paula, fights never last long.*

How did you reply? My God, you children really can be so cruel to each other.

After working on the central area, Michèle, still full of energy, moves on to the aisles on each side of the nave. She stops in front of a large bouquet of flowers lying on the floor in front of one of the side chapels. The glimmer from the candles and the wan glow of the streetlights through the stained-glass windows create a chiaroscuro that's worthy of a Renaissance master, and Michèle sits down for a moment to take in the still life in front of her before getting back to work. In the total silence, every gesture, every sound – however small – reverberates around the church. *Alexandre, how can you expect to pass your exams if you're always studying with your headphones on? Go to your room, where it's quiet.*

An hour later she takes off her smock, puts the bucket back where she found it, smooths a strand of white hair back into her bun, and puts on her watch and coat. Before leaving, she blows out the three candles. *Goodnight, my little angels of the night. See you tomorrow.* The key safely back in its hiding place, she takes the same route in the opposite direction, encountering only two or three people in the twenty minutes it takes her to get home. After a quick cup of herbal tea, which she drinks standing in the kitchen with her back against the counter, she undresses, puts on her thick, floor-length nightdress and slips into bed as quietly as she can, so as not to wake her husband.

Wednesday, 4.30 a.m. *Shit!* That's the first thought that pops into Lena's head when she looks at her alarm clock every morning – or night, depending on how you look at it. For Lena 4.30 a.m. is always the start of her day. She'd gladly hurl the wretched clock across the room, but she's afraid she'll wake her little brother, who's dreaming happily in the bunk above her. Lena extricates her long, skinny body from the covers, picks up the faded one-clawed stuffed toy crab off the floor and slips it under François's arm. She heads for the bathroom, kicking out at the miaowing cat who wants to rub himself against her legs and sending him flying. *Out of my way.*

'Is that you, Lena?' asks a drowsy voice. 'What in the world are you doing?'

'Nothing, Mum. Go back to sleep.'

She studies her pale face in the mirror and adds a provocative shade of red to her full lips. Satisfied with the result, Lena returns to her bedroom to get dressed. A barely there pair of denim shorts over black tights. She hesitates for a moment, then opens the window. As an icy gust of wind bursts into the room, she changes her mind and swaps the shorts for skinny trousers with ripped knees. On her way out she grabs her coat and backpack. It's still too early for the Métro, of course – train drivers, like everyone else, are still tucked up in bed. But she's used to it, so she powerwalks to the café. At this hour, which is neither fully day nor night, strange characters appear out of the city's woodwork. The party-goers have already gone home, and the early-morning shift workers aren't up yet. Which only leaves a few haggard homeless people who regularly sleep in the streets. Though it's not much of a sleep, disturbed as it is by noises, smells and the cold, and haunted by fear. Their faces, which can only be seen clearly when close up, look wild. Sometimes one of these figures will suddenly loom out of the shadows, bluntly demanding money or a light. But Lena is never afraid. For her, this snatch of time before the orderly world wakes up offers a welcome distraction from her problems.

She arrives at the café at exactly 5 a.m., just as the red neon sign comes on, its letters reflected on the wet pavement.

Lena says hello to Franck, the café owner, whose appearance never changes. His tattooed arms, bursting out of a skintight T-shirt, are permanently on display whatever the weather, and he always has a silver chain around his neck. She sets up the chairs, none of which match, while he takes care of all the important stuff. She runs her hand over a grimy-looking table and turns up her lip in disgust.

'The night shift team doesn't do any cleaning then?' she asks wryly.

Without a word, Franck throws her a damp paper towel. Lena mutters under her breath as she wipes away the crumbs from the night before, then settles in at the bar with her elbows on the counter. Franck waves a basket of warm croissants under her nose, but Lena immediately pushes them away.

'You'll fade away if you're not careful,' he warns.

'Just a cup of coffee, please.'

Franck sighs as he tries in vain to find a radio station with good reception. Nothing but static. Lena watches him with an amused expression on her face.

'Good morning, everyone!'

It's Amar, the only other person who regularly calls in this early. He's drowning in an oversized leather jacket, his faded jeans practically falling off.

'You all right, Amar?' asks Lena.

'I'm all right. Slept good.'

'It's "slept well", Amar. "Slept good" isn't how you say it.'

'Come on, lay off him,' Franck intervenes.

Amar has lived in France for twenty years, in a little room above the café, which Franck lets out to him at a rent that's below the market rate. Lena likes him, maybe because of his accent and grammatical mistakes. They remind her of the ones her paternal grandparents make, although she hasn't seen them for five years. Not since they stopped making the trip to see her and François. They're too old and frail now.

She'd like to visit them, but her mother can never afford the plane ticket. She finishes her coffee in silence, then steps behind the bar to find something better on the radio. Returning to her stool, she pulls her course notes out of her bag and begins to study them. At six-thirty, the bin men turn up, quiet time over. This is when she goes home to see François off to school before she heads off to her class. Every morning she goes out of her way to make him a breakfast fit for a king.

Thursday, 10.18 p.m. Hervé closes his book and turns out the light. He's exhausted and, despite previous experience to the contrary, at this moment he still believes it's perfectly possible that he will fall asleep as soon as his head hits the pillow. Surely, tiredness has to get the better of him at some point? And perhaps tonight is the night. But tonight is never the night, and after a period of hope during which he feels close to victory, his thoughts catch up with him. Nothing extraordinary – just what he did earlier, what he has to do tomorrow, and how he has the yearly accounting to finish, with the whole agency relying on him to get it done on time. The meeting is in six weeks, which will go by quickly. He stops to reflect on how pointless it is to worry, then starts worrying again. Christmas will soon be here, and with it the annual dinner he has with his son. How old is he again? Twenty-five? Twenty-six? His birthday is in December – of that much Hervé is certain, but he always has to think for a while before he can pinpoint the exact date. And that in itself speaks volumes. What should he buy him? He must improve on the pathetic attempts he's made for the past few years. Hervé wants his son to see him as a proper father, rather than the shell of a man he feels he is at the moment. He doesn't want to let down the agency either. The people there have always been kind to him, even though he has nothing in common with them. There they are, elegant and successful, in their fashionable outfits. Always knowing how to make people laugh and ensure their voices are heard. Oh so at ease wherever they go. While he, by comparison, barely even exists. His conversations with them, which are few and far between, are reduced to basic information and barebones niceties. He eats his lunch at his desk and never even dares to go to the office canteen, but brings a flask of coffee from home instead.

Hervé knows that behind those smiling faces, that relaxed demeanour and all those compliments on his work lies a steely inflexibility and he lives with this pressure all the time. He keeps coming back to that seemingly innocuous comment his boss made in the corridor one day. Trying to find the hint, the hidden meaning. 'How are you, Hervé? You seem tired. Careful, we're counting on you, you know!' What did it mean? Was it a warning? That 'careful' filled him with dread. Given how much the agency has grown, he thinks, he could really use an intern to help out. This job is the only thing he knows how to do well, and now he's starting to worry about the impact his lack of sleep is having on his work. It's getting harder and harder to remember the simplest bits of information, and accomplishing even everyday tasks seems to take what feels like a superhuman effort. Things that used to be simple are no longer so. His pulse races and Hervé places his hand over his heart. He needs to think about something else. After all, there's no reason to believe he'll fail. So far, he's always been able to manage his tiredness. And now he has the meetings – that's why he signed up to them. Things will get better . . .

11.10 p.m. He knows he shouldn't, but he picks up his smartphone from the bedside table to check his inbox. He doesn't have to do it, but he knows he would feel guilty if the agency were to send him an important email and he didn't reply. He is aware that some of his colleagues stay late, often happily spending the night at the office. He sees them when he arrives in the mornings, parading their exhaustion, proud of their ability to put their lives on hold for their jobs. Their salaries are nothing like his, of course. Phew, no emails. Hervé breathes a sigh of relief.

I'll try a little bit longer, he thinks to himself, glancing at his alarm clock. It's always around this time that he wonders how it is that a full day of work doesn't lead, naturally and seamlessly, to restful sleep; to a night so revitalising that it will make a new man of him – a man ready to spring out of bed in the mornings, his head held high. Instead of which he has grown more feeble and tired with every passing year.

He switches his attention to the sound of the leaky tap in the bathroom. *Drip, drip, drip.* Now he can't block it out. Every drop of water sounds louder and louder as it hits the ceramic shower base. The flat's ancient pipework regularly disturbs his sleep (and his mental health), but the very thought of calling the landlady – or rather her son – terrifies him so much that he prefers to suffer in silence. His tiny flat, comprising a narrow hallway, postage-stamp-sized kitchen, and a main room with a bed, dining table and sofa, belongs to an old woman. The floral wallpaper and thick velvet curtains are vestiges of her life here. Now that she's in a retirement home, her son manages the flat. Well, 'manages' is putting it rather generously as he refuses to spend a penny to do the place up, but still raises the rent every year. The law is on Hervé's side – he could demand that the wiring be brought up to standard so he doesn't have to worry about electrocuting himself every time he touches a light switch – but the landlady's son is so difficult that the very sound of his voice makes Hervé want to hide. Anyway, no one ever visits, so he does what he can himself, here and there, and somehow it all holds together.

1.00 a.m. He knows he won't fall asleep now, so he climbs out of bed. He takes off his worn old pyjamas and grabs his corduroy trousers, shapeless grey jumper and tweed jacket – all strewn carelessly on the floor at bedtime, back when he was still full of optimism. (It's an empty optimism, admittedly, but one that is necessary for his survival.) When his thoughts really start to get the better of him, he goes outside to avoid the panic attack he knows is coming, the kind that leaves him feeling as if he's going to die. A racing heart, shortness of breath, profuse sweating, numbness in his extremities . . . he gets all the symptoms. One night he decided he deserved to take back some control over his dismal nights. And once he'd made up his mind, he found he enjoyed strolling the streets aimlessly, letting the night take him where it pleased. Walking under the artificial glow of the streetlamps, he felt himself slipping into a soothing anonymity.

Friday, 1.30 a.m. All my senses are on full alert. I listen attentively to a distant howl. Somewhere between the worlds of dreaming and wakefulness, I'm not sure if I've imagined it. But my anxiety is certainly real.

'Paul, can you hear that?' I ask, frightened. 'It sounds like a wolf.'

'Yes. It's nothing – probably just an owl. There aren't any wolves here. Where do you think you are? Go back to sleep.'

Go back to sleep . . . I would have to have been asleep in the first place. The fact that he's asleep annoys me. Other people sleeping has been getting to me for a while now.

The perfectly round moon lights up the room like a film

projector. I watch it, along with the dark canopy of trees, from my bed, my head propped up slightly on my pillow. Just thinking about the distance there is between me and that white sphere makes my head spin. But for the moment this sole source of light in a sky that is as black as it is bottomless has a hypnotic hold over me. The howling starts up again. Without sunlight the world outside becomes a hostile jungle full of unexpected dangers. A muffled creak pulls me out of the light sleep I'd fallen into. I leap out of bed. It's coming from the attic. A load-bearing beam is about to give. The house is going to collapse around us . . . I think about waking Paul for a second time, but I know he won't go and check it out. Then, just as I'm about to drift off again, another sound – quieter this time – pulls me back. I would give anything to be able to sleep alone – anything to not have to listen to this constant insidious snoring. I've lost count of the number of hours I have spent like this. Lying next to men who blissfully snore away, dead to the world, while I am wide awake on the other side of the bed, eyes jammed open and feeling spinelessly abandoned. And totally alone. At times like this, I have often dreamt of grabbing all my things and sneaking away. I might as well be on my own properly. If only I were brave enough . . .

I remember having the same feeling of loneliness as a child – stuck in my bedroom in our family home, which was hidden in the middle of a huge garden that was so overgrown it looked like a jungle (my parents having neither the time nor the inclination to look after it). I can still see myself lying perfectly still in bed for hours, staring at the glow-in-the-dark stars that were stuck to my ceiling. My mother has often told me there never *were* any luminous stars in my room. (That said, she spent so little time there that it's possible she simply failed to notice them.) And it's true, I don't have any memory of her or my father on a stepladder. So who put them up?

My mother thinks I imagined them. Perhaps she's right. My memories are so vague . . .

My nights are like a child's, full of unfounded fears and worrying shadows. And that's despite all the thought and effort put into decorating and furnishing our bedroom. By day, the bed is a welcoming invitation to rest. It sits in the middle of a large bright room and is neither too wide nor too high, neither too hard nor too soft. It's covered in cushions and blankets that are made of carefully selected natural fabrics. The furniture doesn't take up too much space, and every mark of wear and tear tells a story. I searched for ages before deciding on the bedside lamps, which cast the perfect amount of light for reading in bed, without being too bright. I wanted to make my bedroom a warm and loving body to cuddle up against. But when night falls and the lights are out, the illusion disappears, and I might just as well be in a prison cell or quarantine room.

4.30 a.m. The howling has stopped, but the silence is even worse. Nothing is happening now and all the attention I focused on the noises outside is zeroing in on me. I can feel my heartbeat speeding up to match my racing thoughts. I pick up my mobile from the bedside table. The home screen offers up a selection of headlines, sordid crimes and other serious and disturbing topics. I get lost here, in these pages that I don't even have to turn.

5.30 a.m. The treetops disappear in the mist that's floating through the air at the far end of the garden. My thoughts calm down, my breathing eases, and my muscles relax. I finally fall asleep.

7.30 a.m. The hot water is soothing. I'm sitting with my knees pulled tight against my chest. I don't have the strength to stand. I'm running out of time, but I can't bring myself to leave my warm bubble. I can't move. I pass the shower head over my huddled body, alternating between my neck and my chest as I watch the streams of water trickle along the curves of my body and disappear into the folds of my skin. Seeing my body like this is a painful reminder of how a lack of physical affection has dried me out, like a dead branch. Turning off the tap demands a willpower I don't have. The shivers that will torment me before I can get dried and dressed seem insurmountable. Paul's deep voice calls out to me, firm and unyielding. I close my eyes, as if to block out the sound coming from the bottom of the stairs, but it grows louder and harsher. We're going to be late. He has to go, and Thomas still isn't ready. What on earth have I been doing in the bathroom for the last half hour? Do I think I'm the only person living in the house? *Leave me alone*, I want to scream at him. *Just forget about me for one minute. Give me time to gather my thoughts before going out into the wild, heartless world.* He knows perfectly well that I haven't slept. I want to yell at him, but I keep quiet and stifle my anger. *Don't upset anyone, avoid conflict, do what's expected of you.* I know how to do that. I make a superhuman effort to get out of the shower and endure the shivering.

There's a knock on the door. Not a knock, exactly, more of a gentle tap. As if from someone who doesn't want to disturb. It's Thomas who's come to brush his teeth.

2

Monday, 8.05 a.m. The room is empty, but there's a red note on the whiteboard. *Sleep meeting sixth floor, door at the end of the hall.*

By the time I get there I'm late – again. Though this time I'm not the only one, it seems. Standing in the doorway, I take in these new surroundings. The room looks smaller than the one we had before, but perhaps that's just because it's an attic. The faded walls are lined with old-style Ikea bookcases containing yellowing copies of airport novels, and in the corner a huge man seems to have nodded off in a battered green velvet armchair. He looks dead to the world, so I take this opportunity to study him more closely. Brown corduroy jacket, a navy-blue turtleneck sweater that appears to be cashmere, and pristine dark-blue jeans. He must be the no-show from our last meeting. His face is lit by a lamp fitted with a hand-made paper lampshade, its yellow light contrasting sharply with the grey mist outside.

Despite the ageing furniture, this room has a much better feel to it than the one on the third floor. I walk over to a large attic window with breathtaking views of the sky and the city rooftops but am soon interrupted. Michèle has arrived with Hervé in tow. (They met on the stairs, she explains, laughing.) She's pleased to see the wooden table, where she sets down her wicker basket and pulls out mismatched mugs, a thermos, small silver spoons and a Tupperware bowl of sugar cubes.

I decide to help her – I enjoy her company. I tell her she has the same name as my paternal grandmother, whom I never knew, and she confides in turn that she has always admired the saint *I'm* named after. *Saint Claire* – she says it several times with a smile. There's no doubt her faith is strong – that's obvious from the small gold cross she wears around her neck. And it pains me to disappoint her – I don't know why, but I want this woman to like me – but I feel forced to admit that, despite being taught by nuns, I lost any reverence I might have had for the saints a long time ago. Michèle is about to give an answer to this when Hélène walks in, apologising for being late. She has been held up by an 'emergency'. *What kind of emergency could possibly require a sleep psychologist at this time in the morning?* I wonder.

'You found your way OK, I hope?' asks Hélène. 'So, Claire, what do you think?'

'Well, it's definitely better than listening to children scream next door.'

'Yes, it's certainly quieter but it's not exactly a retirement home. In fact, it used to be a medical centre. This is the room the nursing assistants used for their coffee breaks.'

'Could we make the meetings a bit later? I never get up before eleven o'clock, so getting here by eight is rough,' says the man in the armchair, who, still rubbing swollen eyes above huge dark circles, has finally stirred.

Hervé pulls a strange face, as if he wants to say something but can't. Maybe he doesn't want the time to be changed but daren't say so.

'No, we can't,' replies Hélène. 'Are you Jacques, by any chance?'

The man nods as he gets up from the armchair and slowly makes his way to join us.

Lena, who's just turned up in a denim mini-skirt, torn tights and big boots that must weigh as much as she does, casts a doubtful glance around the room. Her light floral-print jacket doesn't seem to be very appropriate for the season somehow.

'Lovely. The Insomniacs in the Attic,' she jokes darkly.

'It's where the nursing assistants used to have their coffee breaks,' Hélène repeats long-sufferingly. 'And since we're all here today, we can discuss an important tool: your sleep logs. Did you fill them out?'

This woman, along with her sleep logs, is beginning to annoy me. I don't know why – she seems perfectly nice. I think it's her impassive calmness that bothers me. I always find that people who are never flustered make me anxious.

We sit down around the table, where we've already placed our logs as we came in – although 'log' seems a rather lofty term for what is really just some loose sheets of paper containing a chart full of lines and columns. There are lots of little boxes marked with an X or a line, or totally blacked out with scribbles. None of them are legible, except for Hervé's, which have a clarity that's almost soothing to the eye, and Michèle's, which wouldn't be out of place in a calligraphy manual.

Hélène studies each one individually, tiny frowns of incomprehension passing across her face like clouds every now and again. I'm her first target. It's my arrows that are the problem, apparently. I did read the instructions several times, but the chart was still confusing.

Perhaps Michèle will explain it all to me if I ask. Hélène is going over *her* nights now, using her log as a reference. Michèle's insomnia is divided into two precise and distinct time periods – nothing like my hazy, chaotic nights. She goes to bed between two and three o'clock in the morning, wakes up at six, then goes back to sleep from seven to nine. It's the same every night, give or take anything up to half an hour.

'Your boxes are blank until two or three in the morning.

Does that mean you don't sleep at all before then? Not even a little?' asks Hélène, surprised.

'I always find something to do when I'm not sleeping,' Michèle replies evasively.

How can someone who seems so utterly serene suffer from insomnia? I think to myself. I've always seen sleep problems as a symptom of something deeper – neurosis, the heavy toll of responsibilities society saddles us with, a restlessness of mind, perhaps. But Michèle seems all clear on those fronts. As I study her discreetly, trying to work all this out, Hélène moves on to Lena, and, again, is surprised by her routine – in this case her daily wake-up time of 4.30 a.m.

'And you go to bed at eleven? That's not much sleep at all. Have you tried going back to sleep afterwards?'

'I've never been able to since . . .' mumbles the teen, hiding behind her hair.

'Never . . . since what? Since when?'

Lena stammers out the fact that her father always used to get up at that time to go to work. Hélène, who can see the girl is struggling, doesn't push her for more details, just suggests – gently and very much in passing – that it might be better if she stopped filling in her log with moons and suns, so that it's easier to read.

There's something about this public dissection of our insomnia that makes me uncomfortable. I know it's all done with the very best of intentions, but just hearing Hélène go through every detail of our sleepless hours out loud like this feels like a violation of our privacy. I watch as Hervé nervously pushes his small round glasses up the bridge of his nose and suspect he's rather nervous as he waits for his turn. The psychologist's voice is gentle, but a wave of panic washes over his thin face when she asks him what he does between one and four o'clock every morning, since these boxes have all been left blank. Before Hervé can answer, the silence is broken by the sound of snoring. Jacques is asleep with his head in his hands.

They should leave him be, Lena whispers, but Michèle disagrees: it would be a waste if he missed out on a session. Hervé, who's grateful for the distraction, suggests it would be a shame to wake an insomniac. I call for a vote.

'JACQUES!'

Hélène's voice cuts through our indecision – and Lena's indignant glare. The large man wakes up with a start and without further ado, Hélène starts going through his log. He goes to bed at ten o'clock every night and dozes until midnight. After that, it all gets a bit confusing. This time it's not the arrows that are the problem, as they were with me, but Jacques's use of the letter S, which, confusingly, he has used for 'sleeping pill' and not 'sleepy'.

'Why do you have several "S's" every night then?' Hélène asks, confused.

'I divide my sleeping pills, that's why. Sometimes I take half now, half later, and sometimes I double the dose. It all depends,' he replies, as if it were obvious.

He raises his hand to his head as he speaks, rubbing his eyes with a dejected air. I don't particularly take to him. There's something about that permanent air of cool confidence, that purposefully dishevelled grey hair – university-professor style, with big ego to match – that I find irritating.

'We'll talk more about medications later, and how they can sometimes have the opposite effect to what's intended,' says Hélène. 'But meanwhile, let's carry on looking at your sleep logs.' Looking up, she sees our confused faces and sighs. 'All right, I'll start again.'

Sensing another lecture may be on the cards, I make a huge effort to follow what she's saying. I see Hervé and Michèle are managing to concentrate, but catch Lena discreetly reading a sheet of paper from her half-open binder.

Her homework, I suppose. Hélène is calmly, and yet again, explaining how to use the logs. We're to fill them out every morning to assess our nights, and every evening to assess our days.

'The rows are days and the columns contain the twenty-four hours in each day. You must draw a downward arrow in the box corresponding to the time you go to bed or lie down for a nap, and an upward arrow in the box corresponding to the time you wake up. So the periods when you're actually asleep or awake will be in between the two arrows. If you sleep, fill in the box and if you're awake for a long time, alternate the filled-in boxes with blank ones as you see fit. The letter H means half-sleep and the S means daytime sleepiness, or the times when you feel drowsy. So if, say, you feel sleepy at lunchtime, put S in the relevant box.

My eyes close, then open again. To keep myself awake, I colour in every other box on the graph paper in my notebook, creating an irregular chequerboard.

'So, Claire, do you feel you understand the arrow system now?'

I nod.

'There, now everything's perfectly clear, right?' Hélène concludes, sounding satisfied, then goes on. 'You're all here as a result of what one might call a rigorous selection process. You each filled out a twenty-page form that has allowed me to assess the severity of your insomnia. And your sleep logs will now help me tailor the method to suit each of you individually. You will need to bear all this in mind if I am to achieve the best results for you.'

We are all quiet – a little dazed by this information.

'What method is that then?' asks Lena.

'That will be the subject of our next meeting. But we're done for today. See you back here in exactly two weeks' time. In the meantime, try not to use any screens at least two hours before going to bed.'

The big steel-grey clock on the wall reads 9.05 a.m. Lena leaves first, wearily explaining, as she puts on her floral jacket, that her accounting class starts in less than half an hour. It's the last year of her course, so she can't afford to miss it. Hervé, unfolding his long legs, follows. Michèle is the next to leave. Jacques, who doesn't seem to be in any particular rush, makes his way back to the armchair as Hélène, still sitting at the table, tidies away her notes and her diary. I stand perfectly still in front of the window, my coat in my hand. The constant motion in the sky, the way the sunlight comes and goes, and the infinite shades of the clouds, keep me glued to the spot.

'Don't you work, Claire?' asks Hélène, coat on and ready to go. She's interrupted my daydreaming and is diplomatically asking me to leave.

'I do, I do – I'm just going now,' I reply.

I have a job, and it's time for me to get going if I want to keep it. A dozen proofs are sitting on my desk, waiting to be marked up. I'm a proofreader of downmarket thrillers with totally predictable plots – the sorts of books that horrify people who like a finely rendered sentence. My mother, who has two master's degrees, has never got over the fact that this is what I've settled for. But unlike other jobs I have tried my hand (and failed) at, I know I do it well. There was a time when I even had a go at writing myself and – during periods when I felt my various anxieties were in check – would spend entire evenings, even nights, pouring out words. I felt that I had something to say and hoped people might listen. It was this optimism that led me to draft two hefty novels – both flatly rejected by publishers in letters that were cold, brief and uncompromising. Despite these blows, I wanted to try writing a third book before giving up for good, but I wasn't sure. I didn't believe in writing purely for pleasure and wanted to feel I could make a success of it.

I mentioned it to Paul one day when we were alone together in the garden – he pruning something or other and me lounging on a deckchair. I was secretly counting on some honest words of encouragement that might make me want to start writing again. Something along the lines of *Don't give up, sweetheart, keep trying, persevere, I believe in you.* Not a bit of it. He pretended to be sorry, said it was a shame for me to give up a hobby I enjoyed, then completely changed the subject. And all without even stopping to spare me a glance. I remember looking up at him, devastated by what I'd just heard. It wouldn't have been so bad coming from an acquaintance, or even a friend. But this was Paul – the man I shared my life with, the person who was supposed to know what mattered to me. *A hobby* . . . And the worst of it all was that he had struck a nerve. I knew he was right. I was useless, totally lacking in talent. I went inside, gasping for air. He had unmasked me. How could I have been so stupid as to believe I could be a writer? And – even more embarrassing – a successful one? I blushed with shame. I should have known. Nothing had changed since school. *Not good enough, could do better, just middling.* Despite entire weekends spent studying – it's not as if I had any friends to hang out with – I was never anything but average. I can still remember the disappointment on my parents' faces every time they read my school reports. To save face, I forged another persona for myself – a character of proud indifference – that I honed over the years. A double, if you like. And I've lived with these two versions of me ever since, to the point where sometimes I can't remember which one is real.

I could have told Paul to go and get stuffed or – more reasonably – simply explained how hurtful his reaction was. But I didn't know how to express myself – or my feelings. So I just stood there in the kitchen, like an idiot, trying to hold back my tears. I took up gardening the next day. At least if nothing grew, I reasoned, I could always blame climate change.

As I turn away from the window, I notice the armchair is empty. The large man has left without saying a word.

Monday, 2 a.m. Lying on his back, his arms straight by his sides, Jacques suddenly opens his eyes and stares at the ceiling, where the time is displayed in large red numbers. For months of sleepless nights he had fought the temptation to look, banishing his alarm clock and any other screen that might give him a clue as to the time. But then he gave up. And on the basis that he might as well confront his enemy head-on, installed an alarm clock above the bed that defiantly projects a digital readout of the hours, minutes and seconds on to the ceiling. His laptop is hidden under the mattress and his mobile under his pillow.

He thinks back to the phone, which rang at midnight on the dot. It's always midnight on the dot. It was his office phone. After it rang, he snatched two hours' sleep disturbed by images of charts with filled-out boxes.

He feels like a prisoner in a body that's too small for him. A vice compresses his muscles, his flesh, his skin, his heart. He goes through the list of all the things he could do if only he had the strength to get out of bed. Make himself a cup of warm lemon water, perhaps, and sip it while looking out of the window to see who else in the neighbourhood is awake at this time. (It's always so comforting to see a light on in the building across the road – a sign of companionship in this sleepless solitude.) On a more constructive note, he could think about his handful of patients – the ones who are still lucky enough to be able to see him despite the decision he made earlier in the year to take on fewer cases. (His glory days were behind him. He knew that he was living off his reputation rather than his hard work – the drive wasn't there anymore.) He turns on his bedside lamp – it's a vintage designer one – and looks around his big bedroom, with its meticulously minimalist decor. His wife once read in a feng shui book that an uncluttered environment promoted sleep. Jacques was already having problems even then, though it all seems so long ago. And Catherine did everything she could to find a solution.

The flat is too big now. It's clearly ill-suited to the needs of one person and makes him feel silly. His wife is away most of the time. *When did that start?* he wonders, but he can't remember. He wasn't aware of it at first – it seemed to happen gradually without him noticing. As for his three children, they moved away one by one, and are now scattered across the globe. He wasn't prepared for the loneliness that engulfed him when they left, or the major impact it had on his sleep. Though it wasn't insomnia, he insisted. He couldn't stand the word, much less his wife's tactful suggestions – whenever she was around – that he should get some help.

He thinks back nostalgically to the small one-bedroomed flat they had in the early days before expanding into the rest of the floor as the children were born and his career took off. He had even ended up buying all the attic rooms on the floor above, turning what was once a modest flat into a luxurious maisonette. But now it feels as if each additional square metre has distanced him further from his wife – and, truth be told, from himself.

He doesn't get up. He doesn't do anything, except try to slow down his thoughts. His legs hurt, as if his body has been taken over by a stranger. He doesn't know where to put them. He picks up the second half of the sleeping pill sitting next to the glass of water on his bedside table, swallows it, and closes his eyes. Fragments of conversations with his patients keep him half-awake.

3.30 a.m. He opens his eyes again, grabs the TV remote and methodically surfs his one hundred and fifty channels until five o'clock, the time he generally falls asleep in earnest.

Tuesday, 1.10 a.m. *Paula, go back to bed, I'll be there in five minutes. No, you won't die in your sleep, I promise. No, your friend is wrong, her grandmother isn't asleep forever. She's dead, she's in heaven, and she's in very good company. Yes, Antoine, I'll go there too one day, but not while you all still need me. Go and brush your teeth. Could we get to bed on time for once?*

Michèle meticulously dusts the pews lining the main aisle. Not a single inch of wood, no nook or cranny can escape her beeswax-coated rag. When she's finished, she sits down for a second to enjoy the serenity this place inspires in her. She feels totally safe here. There's no other place on earth that makes her feel so at peace. It's as if the heavy wooden doors of the church protect this sanctuary from the outside world, from everything that is evil, absurd or obscene. *Can I come in, Alexandre? How are you doing, treasure? You've seemed a bit out of it lately. You haven't been talking much. Could you try to keep your brother and sister from fighting too much? Your father will be home late. I know, but it's his job. We can't be cross with him.*

She looks at her watch. She's running late tonight. I'd better hurry, she thinks. If it's too late, I won't be able to get to sleep. She's convinced she can't fall asleep after 3 a.m. She believes it so fervently that the thought has become a reality.

She quickly puts away her materials, writes a little note, which she leaves on the desk, and puts away her smock.

Later, when she gets into bed, she resists the temptation to wake her husband to tell him about her evening. It's such a pity he doesn't understand.

Wednesday, 5.05 a.m. Lena shivers as she waits outside the shuttered café. She could have stayed at home, where it's warm, but once she's up, she can't help it, she has to get out of the house.

'Franck, when you run a café, you show up on time. Especially when it's raining.'

'Don't fret, sweetheart. Maybe you should dress more warmly. Here, open up instead of complaining. I have to go get the bread. Jesus, it's cold out.'

Lena opens the finicky locks, then turns on the lights and makes her way behind the bar. She loves it when Franck leaves her in charge. It makes her feel important and she struts around like a queen.

'Hi, Amar,' she says as the regular walks in.

'A pastis, please, honey,' he says casually.

'Do you think I was born yesterday?' Lena asks, her eyebrow raised. 'Franck never serves you alcohol before ten o'clock.'

'Fine, a cup of coffee then,' he concedes.

Franck arrives, his arms laden with warm baguettes, and Lena is demoted to simply being a customer again.

'Hey, Franck? You know it's almost Christmas, right?' she asks.

'You're getting ahead of yourself. It's only November,' he counters.

'OK, but have you given any thought to what your café looks like every year compared to all the other cafés and shops round here?'

'If you don't like it, you can go home and go back to bed.'

'Don't take it personally, but you have to plan ahead for this sort of thing,' she continues.

'When your customers come here in the morning, feeling knackered and fed up, they really want to see a tree, some tinsel and lights, you know? They need that in their lives. It sounds stupid, I know, but it does them good.'

'Girl right,' offers Amar.

'The girl is right, Amar. We say "the girl is right". Jesus, you can't just leave off the verb!'

'Lay off him! What do you care?'

Amar smiles, his face bent over his coffee cup.

'What makes you think I can afford decorations anyway?'

'I know you can't. But I have a whole load of them at home. Boxes of them. My dad used to get them out every year to decorate his shop windows.'

'Go ahead then, if it makes you happy,' concedes Franck. 'Just don't knock any holes in the walls.'

Lena's still thinking about all the ways she could decorate the shabby café to make it worthy of a movie set when Franck waves a piece of buttered toast under her nose. She pushes it away, a look of disgust on her face.

'It's only bread.'

'I've told you before, not sleeping kills my appetite.'

Lena takes out her notes and starts studying on the counter. Her mock exams are just before Christmas, and she knows she's already on dangerous ground, but she can't concentrate for more than half an hour at a time. As soon as she sits down in class, the urge to sleep becomes irresistible, and the teacher's words fly right over her head. She's been called to the head's office countless times for her lack of attention. She was so close to passing last year. She missed getting her diploma by just a few points – if it weren't for that she might already be working in a big bank or a fancy international law firm.

Thursday, 1.34 a.m. Hervé is sitting at the back of the café. He likes it here because it's a total contrast to the fashionable places that partygoers normally love. It took him a while to find it. He spent hours online researching cafés and bars that were open after two o'clock in the morning, then staked them all out. It didn't take long to sift through them and discover this was the only one he liked. Every time he walks in, he can feel the weight immediately lift from his shoulders. The pale complexions and dark undereye circles of the customers hunched over their glasses have become a familiar sight, though he's never tried to get to know any of them or strike up a conversation. He somehow doesn't feel it would be a particularly interesting exchange. Two or three eccentric night owls, who seem to be permanently locked in the same endless debate, have shot him welcoming glances in vain. The waiters leave him alone and don't even bother with the usual small talk about the weather. Every night he orders the same dish and the same wine – the cheapest on the menu. They serve him with a polite greeting, and he thanks them softly, his voice hoarse from fatigue. Sometimes he falls asleep, and no one is surprised.

People's faces always seem softer in artificial light, Hervé thinks. The darkness makes them more vulnerable, somehow, more sympathetic. The differences that are so glaring in broad daylight fade away here. When he gives up on fighting to sleep in his tiny flat, this nocturnal habitat, this dark world, is where he feels most at ease and most accepted. The visible signs of exhaustion, which he can no longer hide, and which make him look so strange and ghost-like, can seem suspect to those who sleep through the night without a second thought, but here, it doesn't matter.

He takes his sleep log out of his folder and conscientiously fills out the daytime boxes. The third meeting is on Monday. He hopes he won't have to talk too much. He might almost feel at home if he didn't have to talk. All he ever wants is to go unnoticed. Why are people always asking him to speak? The other group members intimidate him, but then again, in his sad life, the only things that don't intimidate him are his spreadsheets. The agency. He looks at his mobile. No emails. They wrote to him at midnight once, in a panic, while wrapping up a proposal for an international ad campaign. But that night, of all nights, he had been asleep, as he miraculously is from time to time. He read the email in the early hours of the morning. And when he arrived at the office with a hardened dread in his stomach, he felt their reproachful eyes on him. He knows he must tread lightly. These veiled barbs – so much worse than clearly worded threats – are a permanent worry.

The yearly meeting is in a month's time. He'd better stay on top of things. The yearly accounts are in order, but he still needs to prepare the summary, which, unfortunately, he's required to present.

He thinks about Claire. He can't work her out – she's made quite an impression on him, but he's not sure why. He finds her pretty, with her big dark eyes and snow-white skin. And she has great style – she could be twenty years old in those jeans and that duffle coat. But then he's always studied other people's charms from afar. Beauty was not for him. Even his marriage was something of a miracle, or a misunderstanding.

He takes a notebook out of his briefcase and jots down a few words. Not in a row, but in columns. Things he sees and hears.

Friday, 11.30 p.m. The train carriage is deserted. Of course it is. Who else would be heading to my sleepy village at this time of night? After N., the reassuring cityscape gives way to dark countryside. Not a single light to pierce the night. I hate taking the last train, but not as much as I hate spending my evenings in an old stone house at the far end of a village with a population of no more than three hundred. I realised the move was a bad idea when I stood among the packing crates on that very first night in the new house. It was Paul's decision – but then again, he was so persuasive that his choices always became mine as well. To be fair, he still wanted to please me, in those days. Things were good. I was in love, still very much smitten with his charms, and my insomnia had actually got better. But all that changed with the move. Everything about the new house seemed as if it had been deliberately set up to make my insomnia worse . . . The silence interrupted by strange noises, the isolation, the darkness – that irrational fear of death that left a lump in my throat every time I went to bed. The countryside tapped into my deepest, darkest fears, and rekindled them. I felt abandoned, far from everything I knew and loved.

We've lived here for three years now. I have spent three years reliving the loneliness of my childhood, every single night. And almost as long silently resenting Paul for doing nothing to stop the slow decline that is threatening to destroy our relationship, for being ice-cold when I am floundering.

All I can see in the train window is my reflection and that of the depressingly empty carriage around me. I should let myself doze off, close my eyes, but an unexplained tension keeps me awake. The dread in the pit of my stomach grows as the train makes its way deeper into the dark landscape. I remain alert, on the lookout for any danger that might suddenly pounce. Tonight it takes the form of a man in a hoodie carrying a beer can who has appeared out of nowhere and is hailing me in an alcohol-slurred voice.

'Hey, lady, what station was that?'

The air fills with the nauseating smell of his breath. I reply tersely, not wanting to come across as over-friendly. I'm desperate for him to keep walking down the carriage. My prayers are partly answered when he sits down several rows away. He could easily attack me, rape me, slit my throat and leave me for dead. There aren't any witnesses or people to help me. I would die in a suburban train as the rest of the country gets into bed . . . But for now, he is listening to something on his headphones and is tapping out the rhythm on his seat. His legs are fidgeting. Anxiety, perhaps? Or is it drug withdrawal? As I think of all the possible solutions that are open to me, the train slows down and the knot in my stomach jumps up into my heart. The train stops. The forest on either side of the tracks is dense, black and impenetrable. I swear silently to myself, though it's more of a scream inside my head. How can there be problems with the train at this time of night, in the middle of nowhere? And no driver to make a soothing announcement on the loudspeaker, no voice in this carriage to reassure me that someone else is around? It seems he's abandoned me as well. The man, who's removed his hoodie now, looks up and mimes drinking a toast with his can of beer. 'Bad luck, huh? Fucking trains. And they make us pay for them. Bastards. I'd kill them all.' I smile sheepishly to avoid offending him. He suddenly seems very angry. I close my eyes and try to relax my breathing. Time, which seems to have stopped with the train, has my chest in a vice. The man is standing up now, stumbling towards me. I calculate my chances of making it out alive. I'd have to get past him to sound the alarm. He opens his mouth, no doubt intending to produce an obscenity or two, but nothing comes out. He gives up. Too much effort, or maybe it's just my lucky night. He simply waves vaguely, then makes his way to the next carriage, disappearing into the far reaches of the ghost train, which finally starts moving. I let myself breathe again.

When I step out onto the platform, the cold feels like a

slap on my face, making my whole body tremble. I walk quickly, trying to warm myself up. I'm halfway home when the streetlights go out. Of course, it's midnight. I swear under my breath as I fumble with the torch on my phone, and the fear catches up with me again. What if the man got off the train without me noticing? I still have half the village to walk through before I get to the dirt path covered with branches so tightly knit that it feels like a tunnel, shutting out the night sky. I think about calling Paul to come and get me. But no, he'd say I'm being silly. I can just hear him now, *For God's sake, you're not five years old, are you?* I take a deep breath and push on through the narrow streets lined with seemingly empty houses. I'm as terrified as if I had been left in the forest on a moonless night.

The lounge is pitch black. A pity. I would have liked to chat a bit, to let off the tension of the walk home. Paul and I are like ships in the night, these days – we never see each other anymore, just cross paths. I walk over to the wood stove in the centre of the room and warm my stiff hands as I watch the wood crackle through the glass.

I decide to go up, knowing already that I won't fall asleep. As I pass Thomas's room, I stop to look at him for a moment as he lies there, all snugly wrapped up in his bedclothes. I plug in the nightlight that Paul forgot to turn on and carefully remove a dozen toy cars from under his pillow. I stand there, watching the boy sleep for a long time, as if he might hold the answer to the mystery of life, then reluctantly head to my room. I wish I could turn the lights on and read for a while, but Paul would get angry.

I begin my nightly planning ritual. It's 1 a.m. If I sleep from 2 a.m. to 6 a.m., even if I wake a few times between, I'll be able to work normally all morning. If it's any later, I'll struggle unless I can go back to bed once Paul and Thomas have left the house. But that's risky – morning naps can leave me feeling even more exhausted than a bad night. I have to work tomorrow. I must have several angry emails waiting for replies. I hear Thomas cough. He's been doing that a lot lately. If I have to take him to the doctor tomorrow, there's no way I'll get in a nap. And I don't like the sound of that cough, either. I read somewhere that tuberculosis is making a comeback and that antibiotics aren't always enough to beat it. I check myself: if I carry on like this, I'll have Stage 4 cancer in an hour.

2.10 a.m. *Think about something else.* I pick up my phone, but that's not much better. My anxiety grows with every email I open, and reaches crisis point as I realise just how much work is waiting for me. I make mental lists to try to organise myself: one for work, one for the house, another for my admin. I prioritise my tasks, but all the efforts I make to optimise my time don't make any difference – the length of the lists only discourages me.

2.30 a.m. I go down to the kitchen. Wrapped up in a thick woollen shawl, I open the window that looks out over the garden, which is so dark I can't even make out the trees. I light a cigarette and take a few puffs, wondering why I'm even bothering to try and see in the dark. But I know why. I'm putting off the moment when I have to go back up and listen to Paul's annoying snoring. Strange to think that in the beginning I used to cling to his regular breathing like a lifeline.

The day we first met seems like a lifetime ago now, so long it seems like a dream. It was eight years ago. I was at a party where I only knew the host and was looking for an excuse to sneak out before midnight. Paul saw right through me and, with a grin on his face, got me to stay until 12.05 a.m. His voice sounded kind and fatherly; I found it soothing. He wouldn't let me go until I gave him my number. It took me a while to realise he was trying to flirt with me. I wasn't used to men like him paying me any attention: up until then, I mostly attracted unsavoury types who were mainly interested in themselves. After the rush of the first few months they seemed to forget my existence entirely, which was fine with me, really, since I never fell for any of them. I had a hard time letting Paul in, too, but he was so patient and self-confident that I finally gave in. Why on earth did he choose me? I've never been able to understand it. Maybe he liked the challenge of it. Break through the wall, tame the wild animal, satisfy her need to control things to reassure herself. I introduced him to my parents like a trophy, desperately searching for approval, at last in their eyes. This man, as cultured as he was charming, made me feel as if I was worth something. I had hit the jackpot – all a fluke, no doubt, but I had to make the most of it.

The next day, I am exhausted after my night-long battle. There's no optimism, no hope anymore. All I want to do is draw the curtains and stay in bed all day. For my own peace of mind, I force myself to finish the most urgent things on my list. The rest will have to wait.

3

Monday, 8.10 a.m. That clock is taunting me. As soon as I join the group, Hélène comments on my late arrival, though she doesn't go so far as to scold me. I'm doing the best I can – I don't drive the trains, after all! That said, I know I could have taken an earlier one. I don't know why I have this permanent need to be the naughty student in class. Some sort of revenge against the world, I suppose.

Michèle serves me a cup of tea. I sip it while half-listening to Hélène, who's explaining something in rather a solemn voice. We are here, she says, because we are 'hard-core', incurable insomniacs for whom nothing has worked so far, except for sleeping pills. But that, she explains – looking pointedly at Jacques – is another story. Luckily, sleep restriction may yet change our lives.

A wary silence around the table.

'Er, don't we sleep too little as it is?' Michèle finally ventures.

'Sleep restriction is recognised as a simple and effective technique for insomnia,' Hélène says firmly. 'Trust me, this is my job. Did you fill out your logs?'

She sighs when she sees Jacques's wrinkled piece of paper covered in scribbles – then mine, which is half empty.

'I missed a few nights,' I say lamely.

She looks at me intently, as if she's genuinely trying to understand how on earth that could be possible when she spent so much time at the last session explaining how important it all was.

'May I ask how long you've been an insomniac for,' she asks, explaining to the group that it can often be helpful to know how and when the problem started. The story behind my sleepless nights isn't very interesting, but I decide to show willing.

'It started when I was a child. I must have been five years old, maybe younger. I would wake up in the middle of the night in a panic, afraid that I was alone in the house, and would leap out of bed to look for my father, as seeing another person in the house would make me feel better. He didn't sleep any more than I did, so I usually found him sitting in the lounge with a book, or in the kitchen with a cup of herbal tea or sometimes a whisky – I could smell it when I kissed his cheek. I always asked to stay up with him, but he always sent me straight back to bed. A child of my age obviously wasn't interesting enough to share his sleepless nights.'

'You poor little thing,' Michèle murmurs.

'The upside was that I got to stay home from school when my mother felt I hadn't slept enough. Then, at the age of eight, she sent me to a boarding school run by Dominican nuns.'

'That can't have been much fun!' Michèle responds again, this time with a chuckle. She's obviously had some first-hand experience of nuns.

'Actually, they were more affectionate than my parents! There was a sister who was on duty at nights and was happy to let me wander about until the morning if I couldn't sleep. She was very kind, always squeezing my shoulder or kissing my forehead. I think that helped.'

'How did you keep up in class?' asks Lena, troubled.

'It wasn't easy but somehow I scraped together marks that were good enough to pass.'

'So, your father was an insomniac. That's interesting,' Hélène remarks, mulling over this new information. 'The role of genetics in insomnia is forming an important part of current research.'

She turns back to me but can see from my blank gaze that she's lost me.

I wasn't the only one in that big house with sleep problems, but nevertheless I felt there was no one to help me. My parents were intellectuals, both Theology professors – always off to seminars or speaking at conferences. They shouldn't have had children. I never felt they had any room for me in their lives. Even if they had, I don't believe that I would have filled it to their satisfaction. It didn't take me long to decide that I was surplus in their relationship. They were enough for each other. They had better things to do than to give up their scholarly pursuits to pay me any attention. Bedtime stories were often forgotten and cuddles were all too short. Tenderness clearly wasn't part of their emotional repertoire. I spent most of my evenings with babysitters of varying abilities. I often wondered where they found them. One night the girl that was supposed to be looking after me simply disappeared. I woke up as usual, but no one was there. There was a note on the table in the hallway, but I couldn't read it. I remember waiting for my parents, huddled in a ball in front of the door, not quite believing I'd ever see them again. You could wake up in the middle of the night and find yourself alone in an empty house. It was that simple, and that terrifying. My sleep, which was already fragmented, got worse from then on. My mother tried to reassure me in her own way, mostly by telling me every morning that I'd have plenty of time to sleep when I was dead. But my callow mind hardly found such words reassuring.

Things quickly got complicated from then onwards. By day, at school, I didn't dare get close to anyone, so convinced was I that I was unlovable that anyone who was interested in me would soon realise their mistake. Alone in my gang of one, I couldn't get hurt. At night it was best to stay awake, since, according to my mother, being asleep was the same thing as being dead.

I can see that for my parents sending me to boarding school was the easiest solution. A few years ago, when I plucked up the courage to tell my mother how abandoned I'd felt at being sent away, she nearly choked. How could I think such a thing? It was hurtful. My father adored me. As did she, of course. Boarding school was meant to help me because I was struggling at school. End of story. I apologised. Perhaps I had exaggerated a little. Of course, my parents loved me.

That's the problem. I never know which memories to trust – the ones based on feelings or the ones based on facts.

A large, yellowing poster on the wall suddenly catches my eye. A palm tree, blue skies, turquoise water. The typical kind of poster you see in travel agents' windows that's designed to sell bespoke, yet strangely empty, dreams.

'Listen up,' Hélène continues. 'I've carefully studied your logs from the first two sessions and I'd like to try something. I'll go around the table.'

The atmosphere is tense, our faces worried, as each of us, in turn, is deprived of an hour's sleep – or even two if we're really unlucky. For an insomniac, that's hard to accept. Needless to say, Hélène has chosen to ignore the filled-in boxes from our logs – the boxes that show when we actually sleep.

Lena is first. She has to give up her first hour of sleep. Rather than going to sleep peacefully at eleven o'clock – lucky girl – she'll have to wait until midnight.

'But, Hélène . . .' she says, jumping to her feet.

'It's the best way of delaying your wake-up time.'

'But . . .' she objects again.

'Let's keep any questions till the end of the session, Lena.'

The poor young woman sits back down, a childlike frown darkening her face.

Michèle doesn't fare any better. It's goodbye to that two-hour morning nap she relies on so much.

'If all goes to plan,' explains Hélène, 'you should be going to bed earlier in no time.'

Always dignified, Michèle nods in agreement, seemingly unoffended by this punishment. It's me who can't hold back about what seems to me to be an utterly barbaric system.

'I understand your concerns, but this is the best way of shifting your circadian rhythm, so that you start to sleep at night rather than during the day. By restricting the hours you are allowed to sleep, your sleep quality will improve. It's not a punishment. You're here to relearn how to sleep.'

'Don't worry, Claire. I knew what to expect,' Michèle reassures me.

'My mum didn't say anything about this,' grumbles Lena. 'Now I know why.'

'She signed you up against your will?' asks Hélène.

'Sort of. I fainted during class. She told the doctor I don't sleep enough, and he gave her the forms. Franck helped her fill them all out.'

'Well, you're here now, so let's do our best to reach our goal,' replies Hélène, showing no interest in who Franck might be.

It's me next. Given the mess that is my sleep log, she admits it will be complicated, but decides to give it a go anyway. As a result I'm not allowed to go to bed for any reason whatsoever before 1 a.m., and I have to get up the first time I wake up, even if it's only five o'clock. I start to wonder what's keeping me here. Is it because it would feel cowardly to give up before I've even started? No, that's not it. There's something else too. Despite my initial misgivings about coming, when I look at these four people whom I barely know sitting around the table, when I listen to them revealing intimate parts of their lives through their sleep logs, I'm touched by their familiar vulnerability. Even Jacques must be hiding some weak spots behind that bullish exterior. I'd like to meet Lena's mother, to work out how it can be that she doesn't seem to care that her daughter leaves the house wearing heavy make-up and outfits that couldn't be more provocative, yet is worried enough about her to take the time to enrol her in this group. And how can a man of Hervé's age lack so much presence, and always look so lost? What's the story behind that face, ravaged by anxiety yet softened by childlike curls? What does he do when he's not asleep? They've all begun to interest me. And after all, I probably don't have anything to lose by sharing my insomnia with them.

Hélène moves on to Hervé. 'Do you take a nap every day?' she asks him.

'I'm allowed one at work,' he replies. 'They're very understanding.'

'What nice colleagues you have!' offers Lena, surprised. 'But where do you sleep?'

'In what we call the relaxation room. After lunch, it's reserved for me.'

'I didn't know people could sleep at the office . . .'

'The world of publicity is quite different to a lot of workplaces. I'm an accountant in an advertising agency.'

Amazed by this information, Lena is suddenly intrigued by Hervé.

'What kind of course do you have to do to work at a place like that?' she asks, her curiosity piqued.

'Lena, please don't give up what you're doing. I just wanted to explain that—'

Hélène interrupts Hervé and tells him he must give up his naps and go to bed an hour later.

I'd never heard Hervé string so many words together before. Granted, he was wringing his hands as he spoke, but, still, I think he's beginning to feel at home.

'Jacques, it's your turn. JACQUES?'

Jacques is dozing in his chair, his eyes half-shut.

'Jacques, you must stop using sleeping pills,' Hélène warns. 'You can't stay awake.'

'I'm usually asleep at this time of day. I'm functional from noon onwards. Never before,' he replies disinterestedly.

'Don't you have patients in the mornings?'

'That would be a disaster.'

'Are you a doctor?' Michèle asks politely. 'My husband is a retired doctor.'

'A psychiatrist,' he qualifies with a sigh, as if every word he says requires a superhuman effort.

Lena bursts out laughing. I'm not surprised to hear what he does. I could easily have guessed it. He looks exactly like those psychiatrists you sometimes see on TV – the ones who give their professional opinion on serial killers and other psychopaths. He must really be out of his comfort zone, taking part in these meetings. Hélène studies his log and pieces it all together to see what the pattern is. Bed at 10 p.m. Dozes till midnight. Awake from midnight to 4 or 5 a.m. Occasionally nods off for a bit. Sleeps deeply from 5 a.m. to 11 a.m. Eventually, she issues her verdict. He can't spend his mornings in bed anymore. I imagine him dragging the weight of his body around for hours, summoning up the necessary strength to crawl to the bathroom. Jacques turns to Hélène. I doubt he'll easily agree to do as she says.

'Hélène, the sleeping pills only start working at around five o'clock, and now you want me to get up at dawn? I haven't slept for a year despite all the pills. A few weeks of a so-called sleep log isn't going to change everything overnight. I'm not going to suddenly hop out of bed feeling fresh and full of energy. I'm not trying to be difficult, and I'm willing to make sacrifices, but only up to a point.'

'Very well. We'll take a progressive approach,' replies Hélène. Her natural sense of authority means she's utterly unfazed by anything. 'Start by going to bed at midnight rather than ten o'clock, and we'll see how you get on at the next meeting.'

Without further ado, she turns her back to us and begins to write the fundamental rules of the sleep restriction method on the whiteboard. No TV in the evenings or at night. No computer screens, and especially no mobile phones, for at least two hours before bed because the blue light is bad for sleep. We're to stay out of our bedrooms until bedtime. No alcohol, no tobacco, etc.

A voice pipes up.

'My bed is in my lounge.'

Hélène turns around with surprise. It's Hervé, who's getting bolder by the minute.

'Do you have a sofa?' she asks.

'Yes.'

'In that case, read or listen to the radio on your sofa.'

'The idea is to use your bed only for sleeping,' explains Michèle.

'I have a TV in my room,' adds Lena.

'Put it in the kitchen,' suggests Michèle.

'I'm sure you'll all need to make a few adjustments to make this work,' Hélène concludes. 'I also want to warn you that this technique can cause daytime drowsiness for the first few weeks. I'd suggest you avoid sensitive or monotonous tasks such as driving and so on.'

No one around the table says a word. The anxious silence is broken only by the clinking of spoons in our mugs.

Hélène's voice grows softer as she takes in our confused expressions. 'OK. I can understand your concerns. It's perfectly normal for people with insomnia to worry about making up for lost sleep. Having a nap, going to bed early or having a lie-in are all things that can feel reassuring. But these are precisely the things that must be avoided. Short naps can be wonderful for people with normal sleep patterns, but if you have insomnia, that bit of rest will affect your night-time sleep, which is already fragile. The idea behind sleep restriction is that you sleep less, but enjoy a better quality of sleep. All right, time's up.'

Everyone stays in their seats.

'Michèle, I can make a cake to go with your tea next time. My dad taught me some recipes.'

'That's kind of you, Lena. You're such a breath of fresh air in these meetings. I hope you'll eat some of it yourself – you could do with putting some meat on your bones!'

Lena smiles blissfully. No one has ever called her a breath of fresh air before.

Standing by the door, Hélène is getting impatient. 'I'm sorry to cut you off, but the session is over. And remember: for this to work, you must respect the hours we've set for going to bed and waking up. Consistency is key. I'll see you in a month, once the method has had some time to work!'

Her instructions are drowned out by the racket we all make as we get ready to leave.

Hervé and Lena are already in the corridor. Jacques has stood up, but only in order to get back to the old armchair. As I put on my coat, Michèle puts the mugs away in her basket, then turns towards the armchair and its sleeping occupant. 'Should we let him sleep?' she asks.

'Yes. At least that way we won't be stuck in the lift with him.'

'Oh, he's not so bad,' she smiles.

Before we leave the room, she turns out the lights. In the early morning gloom, Jacques is just a large unformed shape, like a forgotten object. Michèle takes my arm and we head towards the door in silence.

Monday, 11.50 p.m. Jacques gets into bed after finishing a glass of morello cherry juice – his new nightly ritual since reading about the drink's supposedly soporific qualities.

He hears the phone ring and feels the urge to answer. Since

he's not allowed to go to bed until midnight, he might as well find something to do. He makes his way slowly towards the office. The ringing stops when he's halfway across the lounge. Probably for the best, he thinks, as he turns around.

He could have unplugged the damned phone. Catherine had basically begged him to do as much when she saw the negative impact the nightly calls were having on her husband's mood. If he wasn't going to answer it, he should just unplug it! But he always refused. That's when she realised something was wrong. Jacques had never bothered to explain to her that he'd come to embrace the whole ritual. That he found it easier to go to sleep knowing the phone would wake him. It was an appointment he couldn't miss. His former patient was reaching out to him following the disaster that had befallen her more than a year ago. And the fact that it was midnight was no coincidence. One day, during a session, he had broken down and told her about his sleep problems. She had even brought him a little bottle of essential oils. Midnight was symbolic. It was the fateful hour, the hour that marked the point of no return, after which his chances of falling asleep grew slim.

2.30 a.m. He resists the temptation to pick up a screen but takes half a sleeping pill and a quarter of a Lexomil instead, hoping they will calm his nerves.

4 a.m. He attempts to turn on his bedside lamp for the tenth time tonight, but his movement is abrupt and awkward – a combination of irritation and despair – and the lamp ends up in pieces on the floor. It's just as well. He can't help but see it as a sign. The lamp is the only household item he and his wife bought together, in the early days of their marriage. He still remembers how out of place he felt in that high-end designer shop. Now, whenever he walks past an expensive furniture store and sees a couple trying out a sofa, say –

touching it, studying it – it makes him feel sick. It's all so banal, he thinks – a cliche of the typical wealthy couple. How can anyone spend two hours talking about a sofa, go home, talk more about it over dinner, then finally decide to go back and buy it the next day, and feel as if they've actually accomplished something worthwhile? He enjoys nice things and his creature comforts, he won't deny it, but he prefers to just enjoy them without getting bogged down in all the details.

Once home, the lamp displayed like a trophy on one of the rare pieces of furniture they owned at the time, Jacques had made his wife promise they'd never have to do that again. He trusted her taste, so she could decorate the flat as she saw fit as long as she didn't bankrupt them. And so she did, carefully and elegantly. At first, she went to flea markets. Then, as their income grew, she began going to speciality shops. Though Jacques didn't join in, he was immensely proud of their home, which was the epitome of good taste and a haven for well-being. A perfect reflection of their family. Up until a few months ago . . .

He doesn't even know when Catherine is coming home. Tomorrow, perhaps? Next week? She's always between trips and trainings. He seriously doubts she'll notice that the lamp – so laden with symbolism for him – is no more. He probably could have avoided all this by being more considerate, by being a better listener instead of diving into his work and basking in the glory it brought him. In hindsight, he can see he always put himself centre stage in their lives. Everything was about *his* books, *his* conferences, *his* patients. He realised too late that his wife had stopped confiding in him as she had done in the beginning. It had never occurred to him that she might get bored. When their youngest daughter left for university two years ago, Catherine decided to find something more rewarding to do with her time. And now he spends most of his nights alone in their king-size bed.

His first appointment is at noon – he keeps moving them later and later. And he's glad he decided to move his office into his huge flat a few years ago. At first it was to optimize his time, but now it's a relief to have somewhere he can recuperate slowly from his sleepless nights.

He grumbles to himself about the next sleep group meeting. One day, in a moment of weakness – feeling drained after complaining about his insomnia yet again – he'd accepted the form for the sleep clinic that one of his only friends had handed him. He'd filled it out willingly enough, but what had he really expected to gain from it? That he'd find himself philosophising about sleep with top specialists? Instead, he was stuck with a bunch of other losers. Lena was right to laugh. And she probably has no idea just how well-known he is, what with his books and the dozens of patients he turns down. Famous people, too. How did he end up being so lonely that he needs to take part in group sessions?

The patient who regularly phones him occupies his thoughts again. He's had his share of failures, of course, but has forgotten them quickly thanks to his many victories with other patients and his books. But this was a case where a single piece of grit had brought the entire machine to a grinding halt. An emptiness that had been waiting for the right time to emerge had finally done so and taken up residence, invading his lonely and increasingly unbearable nights. He admits his wife was right: his insomnia must have been lurking in some deep corner of his mind for ages.

5.10 a.m. He makes the superhuman effort required to get out of bed. It's the only way to stop the incoherent thoughts that are swirling around his mind. He sits down in an armchair in the lounge with a 'sleepy time' tea, listening for the sounds of the building waking up. Water rushing through the pipes, a door slamming, steps in the corridor. All these noises mean his torture is at an end for now. To feel better about himself, instead of going back to bed as he would normally do, he makes his way towards the bathroom, bumping into every piece of furniture in his path.

Tuesday, 12.45 a.m. Michèle lies in bed staring at the ceiling. After two hours reading in her lounge, she has got into bed, more out of a sense of duty than any feelings of tiredness. Her husband has his earplugs in and is already dead to the world. She had shown him the piece of paper with her new sleep schedule on it and he was relieved to see she was following the recommendations. It's been two weeks since the last meeting, and she hasn't been back to the church. It's been years since she skipped this ritual so maybe she's on the right track? But, as she explains to her husband, despite it all, she's not sleeping any better. 'You will soon,' he says, trying to be as convincing as possible. 'Be patient and you will. The most important thing is that you stay at home.'

1.30 a.m. Her inability to channel her energy reminds her of years ago when she spent entire nights in her bedroom. But that was before she found the church. She tries every position, but it's hard to find the best one for falling asleep. Her joints hurt. To soothe her nerves, Michèle goes through a list of all of the places that make her feel happy. The tiny chapel in the countryside that she likes to visit with her husband. The lounge in her childhood home. Her room at university where she used to stay up late studying. But, despite her best efforts, the three unlit candles keep popping into her head. She says her husband's name out loud. No answer. She has to go.

2.20 a.m. She doesn't bother taking off her coat as she picks up a pile of posters from the priest's desk, then takes out a roll of tape and starts sticking them on the church's inside doors. She lights the candles and a wave of relief washes over her. A deliverance of sorts. She continues with the posters, finally free of the anxiety that has been tormenting her.

No, Paula, of course I wasn't gone forever. What, Antoine? That's silly! The sun won't burn us all up. What have you been watching on TV? I'll have a word with your brother. He just wanted to scare you, that's all. The sun will stay where it is, just like the earth. And I'll always come back every night, because I can't live without you. You light up my long, dark nights. Everything will continue as it should. Forever and always. You and me, together.

Wednesday, 4.30 a.m. Lena puts on her make-up in the bathroom. Her new sleep schedule means extra work is needed to hide the dark circles under her eyes that seem to be taking over her face. Only four hours' sleep now, but she still wakes up at the same time. 'This method's really bloody effective, Hélène,' she mumbles to herself.

'Stop swearing like that,' says her mother, suddenly appearing in the doorway in her dressing gown. 'And you look like a geisha with all that make-up on.'

'A what?' asks Lena.

'Do you want a cup of coffee?'

'I'll have one at Franck's.'

'Come have some hot milk, at least. It's cold outside.'

'Leave me alone, I can't concentrate.'

Ten minutes later, Lena sits down at the table, her eyes smoky and lips blood-red, and watches her mother busy herself in the kitchen. She's aged ten years since her husband left. When she worked in the bakery she wore really unsuitable outfits that showed off her figure – it drove her father crazy. Now she's always in shapeless lounge clothes and has completely let herself go.

The cat hops onto Lena's lap, but she sends him crashing back down to the floor with a flick of her leg. 'I hate that cat,' she says.

'Why don't you sleep, Lena? Aren't your meetings helping?'

'Don't you miss the smell of croissants wafting up to the flat every morning?' asks Lena, changing the subject.

'Don't talk to me about him, love.'

'I'm not talking about him, I'm talking about croissants.'

'What about school? Are you doing all right? You know I won't be able to afford it again next year. You have to get your diploma this year, or . . . And you should eat. The doctor said— '

'I know. Stop nagging me. I have to go, Mum. I have to put up the decorations.'

'What decorations?'

'It's almost Christmas, you know. Ring a bell?'

François bunny-hops into the kitchen. He's abandoned normal walking of late.

'Stop it, François, that's so annoying. Go back to bed. It's too early for breakfast,' says his big sister.

The little boy serves himself a glass of water, then retraces his hops.

'What's wrong with him?' Lena asks her mother. 'That's not normal at the age of seven, is it?'

But her mother's no longer listening. Lena stomps out of the kitchen, annoyed, but once at the door, her bag already on her back, she's suddenly racked with guilt. She turns back towards the little kitchen, barely lit by the light over the stove. Her mother's still sitting there, coffee cup in hand, staring blankly ahead of her because of the drugs she takes, which are supposed to help her feel better. Her worn pink robe is too small for her figure now. Her breasts are so large, thinks Lena, she could nurse half the neighbourhood. Her long, thick black hair has been spared by the passage of time, however – Lena wishes hers looked half as good. She walks over and kisses her mother's soft, round cheek and her mother takes her hand.

'When you were just a few days old he would take you downstairs to the bakery with him so that I could sleep.'

'I know, you've told me a thousand times. I was so plump just from growing up surrounded by pastries that I could have gone without your milk!'

'Dress warmly, sweetheart.'

Before leaving the building, Lena goes down to the dark, dusty basement, despite the repulsion it arouses in her. Luckily, her mother has everything organised and it only takes her a moment to find what she's looking for. Outside, the cold burns her skin. With the box in her arms, her bare hands are fully exposed to the freezing air. That talk with her mother was depressing. Of course, she knows what will happen if she doesn't pass her exams this year. She won't get a third chance, and her whole future will be laid out for her: checkout assistant, cleaner or home help, just like her mother. She's dreamt for so long of being a secretary in a prestigious firm, of helping important executives, but it's still just out of reach. She's even imagined working abroad, in a huge skyscraper, and wearing elegant skirt suits, like the women in American TV series. Her hands are like ice. She runs to the café, which, miraculously, is already open.

'A bit overkeen today, aren't we?' she asks Franck as she walks in.

'I slept here. We hung around after closing,' he replies.

Lena greets him with a kiss on the cheeks. He reeks of a disgusting mixture of alcohol and body odour.

'Can I have a double espresso, please?'

'Shouldn't you be sleeping better thanks to your meetings?'

'Stop going on at me about it. We're trying out a new method, but it's too complicated to explain. Where's Amar? He hasn't been around for days.'

'He went back home, to see his daughter.'

'I'm gonna leave, too, some day. Just you wait,' mumbles Lena under her breath.

Thursday, 10.30 p.m. Hervé is dozing on the sofa. The radio programme he's listening to is unbearably soporific. Since he's not allowed to watch television anymore he's had to make do with highbrow radio programmes filled with monotonous voices. Tonight, it's a contemporary play. He's so tired he wishes he could go to bed right this minute, but Hélène said not before midnight. And Hervé has never disobeyed an order. He places his hand over his heart. His heartbeat is regular. He's been following this new schedule for two weeks now. But, despite all his efforts, his constant yawning hasn't gone unnoticed and at work they've already told him he should go back to napping. The meeting where he has to present the annual balance sheet is getting nearer. It's all he can think about: standing up in front of everyone in the meeting room, surrounded by glass walls. The most dreaded moment of the year. He always doubles his dose of Lexomil a week before. They're always perfectly nice, of course, but Hervé knows they'll sack him for the slightest mistake. And he knows he's not far off making quite a few. His days are not going well. He feels permanently dizzy as he watches the numbers dance on his screen and today it took him three attempts to get through a simple accounting operation. Plus, the guy from sales had to call back a second time to ask for a document he had asked for in the morning. Under normal circumstances, he would never forget to transfer files like this.

He tries to think about something else and turns his attention to the large crack in the ceiling, which was presumably white once, but is now an unappealing yellow. It should have been repainted a long time ago, but there's no point mentioning it to the landlady's son. Hervé has done the maths: even if he did the work himself, the cost of the materials alone would amount to the same as he pays in child support every month. And there's no way around that. His son often says he doesn't need it anymore, but Hervé will never stop sending it. It's symbolic, the one source of pride he has left. He hasn't missed a single payment in fifteen years.

He gets up, takes his sleep log out of his briefcase and meticulously fills it out for the day. They'll be turning them in tomorrow and he's curious to hear how everyone has fared. He thinks of Claire again. She must be married – she may even have children, though he doubts it. He senses a reluctance to fit the mould in her – a need to defy the established rules.

Midnight. After carefully filing away his sleep log, he puts on his pyjamas and gets into bed with a yawn. But during the three minutes it takes him to do this, his tiredness disappears. It's like magic, every night, and he still hasn't worked out how it happens. He spends an hour tossing and turning in bed, trying to get it back, resisting the urge to look at his phone, then finally gives in. He gets dressed and leaves his flat. The café is busier than usual. A woman in a miniskirt and a leather jacket that can't possibly be warm enough for the weather winks at him from the bar. Hervé feels his heart begin to race. In a panic, he declines her invitation with a slight shake of his head. He still remembers the night he spent with one of her colleagues, and it's not a happy memory. He keeps walking until he reaches another one of the establishments on his list – his plan B, of sorts. In the front part of the bar, near the windows that give out onto the street, the mauve walls are lit by neon lights, but Hervé heads for the back, where the light is dimmer, guaranteeing greater anonymity. Here the neon is confined to signs that hang from the walls, casting multicoloured lights on the customers' faces. Music videos play on a huge flatscreen TV. Hervé orders a pint and allows himself to be mesmerised by the images of half-naked singers and dancers shaking their hips in front of luxury homes with private pools.

Friday, 11.50 p.m. The hallway is pitch-black. I walk straight to the kitchen without even taking my coat off and serve myself a glass of wine, which I drink at the window as I smoke a cigarette. I have spent the entire day dragging myself through work meetings I couldn't cancel and fighting off unbearable exhaustion. Luckily, it was my night out with Françoise. She's my only friend. We've known each other since boarding school, where we were both the black sheep in our class. She because of an extraordinarily voluptuous body that our peers couldn't seem to accept, and me because I was so afraid of building ties with anyone that I excluded myself from everything. Happily, however, she was confident and determined, and she decided we would be friends.

In the evenings we would kneel together at the foot of my bed and pray in unison. God was our best friend. Françoise is the kind of person who sends me text messages when she gets home from a party at 3 a.m. to ask if I'm asleep, just because she knows I'm not. Our friendship makes my life better and sometimes even gives me hope. She's still a beautiful woman with nothing but curves, and turns the head of every man who crosses her path. I've always been jealous of the covetous looks she gets. And of her freedom. There are women who are strong like that, as if they were born to determine their own fates and never give in. I belong in the other camp. I'm terrified by anything outside my comfort zone, so will always find plausible-sounding reasons to never venture beyond it.

Françoise is a struggling violinist. Once a week, we meet up for dinner or a classical music concert. Both, if we can afford it.

As for everyone else – acquaintances and more casual friends – I keep my distance. I can't stand listening to their condescending advice about sleep anymore. They always start out being sympathetic, but when things don't get better after a while, they get aggressive. As if the insomnia were brought on by some fault of mine. I haven't gone out to dinner, or any other social occasion, with Paul for a long time. Whenever I did, I was always obsessed with getting home by midnight, which annoyed him, but the truth was that I never really felt at ease in social gatherings. Still, I played my part to perfection, even though I was always bored, out of sync, elsewhere. When I was younger, family get-togethers, birthdays and parties, which I eventually stopped getting invited to, were the worst punishment of all. With Paul I went along with it for years, mostly for the sake of his friends. It was torture, especially when my insomnia was at its worst. Then I put an end to it. He tried to persuade me to change my mind, but that was mostly for the sake of his reputation. The truth is that he was already bored of whatever he had initially found attractive in me and saw me as increasingly unsuited to 'normal life', to the social gatherings he so enjoyed.

I serve myself a second glass and gulp it down.

12.15 a.m. I find Thomas asleep on the floor in a sleeping bag, just inside the door of his room.

'Paul, are you awake? Did you know your son is sleeping on the floor without a blanket?'

'Huh? He wanted to go camping, so I told him to try it out in his room first.'

'You could have put him in his bed once he'd fallen asleep.'

'I'm sleeping . . .'

Pillow talk is a thing of the past for us now. When we first met, Paul had just got divorced and had custody of his six-month-old baby every other week, and we used to spend hours chatting away in bed with tiny Thomas asleep between us . . . But no more. I get into bed and begin my usual nightly ritual. I start by staying still for a few minutes, afraid that moving might stop me from falling asleep. Then I turn onto my right side, then the left. My gymnastics annoy my husband, who abruptly pulls the covers around him more tightly. It's funny how seemingly insignificant gestures can be so full of hostility. Every night I get a long sigh followed by a quick shuffle to the far edge of the bed to get as far away as possible from the disturbance, a.k.a me. He has a gift for making me feel that I'm an annoyance. I'm always searching our past for signs that we were once in love. I make a list of them, then sort them into categories from strongest to weakest. Holidays, surprises, the early days when we moved in together, the difficulties we faced. But I'm forced to admit it was all a long time ago, and that the bond between us has continued to fray over the years. *Will it break altogether one day?* I wonder.

1.00 a.m. I'm utterly exhausted, but there are no signs of sleep on the horizon. My eyes are burning, as they always do after a sleepless night. I prop myself up on two pillows, my arms crossed over my stomach. There's no moon tonight, no stars. Just darkness. It feels as if this place has been deserted by the living. I shiver, unable to warm myself up or relax. I think about the drunken man from the train again. He could be creeping around outside the house, waiting for the perfect moment to break in. Just to get revenge for my standoffishness. 'Your lack of kindness will be your undoing,' Paul said to me once after I'd told off a waiter in a restaurant for who-knows-what. I'd slept particularly badly the night before. Fatigue makes people irritable. No one regrets this side of my personality more than I do. This endless night could swallow us all up, I think. We could wake up in the morning with no light at all. The trees and birds gone, replaced by silence and ashes. Never-ending cold temperatures and a nuclear winter that would slowly but surely put an end to humankind.

The thoughts of death and darkness become overwhelming. When my sleeplessness forces me to imagine my own death or, worse, my mother's, I fall into a bottomless despair. She lives in a tiny village – even tinier than mine – where she moved after my father died, and I rarely go to see her now – no more than two or three times a year. It's always difficult, but I still have an irrational hope that one day something will change – that she'll give me what I need, a chance to finally connect with someone. None of that ever happens, though. After a few bitter exchanges, we fight, and I leave with a lump in my throat, the emptiness as profound as ever.

When I watched them lower my father's coffin into the ground, I felt like an amputee. He'd given me so little, and now he was gone, and had taken a part of me with him. It was unfair, I wanted my due. I had managed to hold back my tears until then, but with the first shovelful of earth, I erupted into sobs, breaking the eerie silence of the occasion. My mother, who wasn't used to seeing me display any form of emotion, lowered her eyes. I think she was embarrassed. An aunt placed a comforting hand on my shoulder, but of course, her kind gesture only made me cry all the more. I received more affection that day than ever before or since. I'm usually so reserved, but I accepted it all – even when it came from strangers – because it felt sincere, and because, for once, I felt as if I deserved it.

I wish I could close my eyes and open them to a bright blue sky. I need this night to end. *Breathe slowly, breathe. Breathe* . . . Whoever came up with this idea that deep breathing is relaxing? Focusing on my breathing only makes me even more anxious. Maybe I should get up and do something useful? Work, for example. I could dig myself out of the hole

I'm in. But I quickly change my mind: if I get up, I'll wake up completely and then I'll never be able to get back to sleep. I glance fearfully at the alarm clock. 3.08 a.m. My heart begins to race. I panic. How will I get through tomorrow? How will I catch up on my work? There are so many proofs piled up next to my computer. I won't even have the strength to make breakfast. I pick up my mobile and scroll through my social network feeds.

I take advantage of the situation to send a reassuring email to a publisher. I realise it's cheeky, but I also know it'll buy me some time.

2.20 a.m. I get out of bed, pick up Thomas off the floor, tuck him into bed, and kiss his forehead. Then I go downstairs for a cigarette.

7 a.m. Over coffee at breakfast I watch Paul and Thomas chat away. Their animated discussion is too loud. Their close relationship feels like a personal attack on me. Sometimes I'm even jealous of Paul's love of his son. They turn to me from time to time, trying to include me in their conversation, perhaps, or even asking me a question, but I can't understand a single word they say. It's as if they're speaking a foreign language. I look at them blankly, alone in another dimension.

When Paul has left for work, I realise he didn't even kiss me goodbye. I need to get dressed. Thomas will be late for school if I don't get moving.

Thomas is fidgety and can't stop talking. I scream at him to be quiet. And I keep screaming even after he's shut up. I want to leave all this behind. After dropping him off at school, I am overcome by a wave of regret. I desperately want to get him out of class, to apologise and give him a huge hug. I'll be angry with myself all day. None of this is his fault.

4

Monday, 7.45 a.m. I took an earlier train and am on time for once. Michèle is sitting in front of a steaming cup of tea in our attic room. She's placed a mug and spoon in front of each chair at the table. She has a thin smile on her face. It's only been a month since we began following our new sleep schedules, and she's already lost some of her radiance.

I'd like to chat with her for a while, but Lena arrives, all smiles as she uncovers the exquisite cake she's made. She puts it down in front of Michèle and waits for her reaction. Delighted by her warm thanks and my praise, she finally takes off her jacket and sits down. The other members of the group file in, followed by Hélène, and we noisily settle in as she begins to go over our sleep logs, eager to see signs of improvement.

Michèle cuts the cake and serves the tea, exchanging a few whispered words with Jacques, who's rubbing his eyes. Huddled on her chair, Lena asks Hervé if he can arrange a meeting for her with the HR department at his agency, because she's having serious doubts about her chosen profession. I smile at him, waiting for his reply, but Hélène clears her throat – a signal that the session has begun. She suggests we start by going around the table, as usual.

Silence.

She turns to Michèle first, surprised at the lack of progress. In fact, if anything things seem to be worse.

'No improvements despite the new schedule? You haven't managed to fall asleep any earlier?' Hélène asks.

Michèle hesitates. 'Well, not exactly. I really tried my hardest, I promise you, to . . . How can I explain?'

'Tried to do what?' Hélène is doing her best to understand.

'To stay in bed at night . . . But it didn't change anything, and I still couldn't sleep, so I thought I might as well go back . . .'

Hélène doesn't react at first – she's too busy trying to decipher the hidden meaning behind Michèle's words. I tot up her hours of sleep in my head and can see there aren't many there. But what does she mean by 'go back'? I wonder. Go back where? Hélène begins to lecture her sternly, reminding her that the reason she mustn't nap in the mornings is so she can get to sleep earlier at night. If she doesn't try, the restriction method will only make things worse. Before moving on, she asks Michèle about her mysterious outings.

'I can't go to sleep when you say I should because I have business to attend to.'

No one says a word.

'You don't work at night, do you?' Hélène is concerned now.

'Oh, no! I'm much too old for that.'

'What sort of business then?' I ask, intrigued.

Michèle hesitates. 'Well, actually . . . I go to church,' she finally admits in what she hopes is a completely normal-sounding voice.

'You go to church in the middle of the night?' asks Lena admiringly. 'Wow, doesn't it freak you out?'

'Quite the contrary, my dear. At night I don't see the darkness, but the dawning of the light.'

I refrain from asking what light she's referring to, though I doubt she means the actual rising sun.

Lena thinks for a moment, then asks, 'Isn't it closed?'

Michèle is embarrassed but she doesn't dodge the question. 'I have the keys.'

'So, instead of sleeping, you go to church?' continues

Hélène, who can't have planned for the session to go down this route.

'I realise it might sound a little odd,' the older woman concedes.

From the moment I first met Michèle I had sensed that there was a free spirit lurking under that conventional exterior but I never would have imagined her sneaking into church in the middle of the night. I'm glad Hélène seems to want to get to the bottom of it.

'Would you mind telling us why?' probes Hélène.

Michèle takes a deep breath. Her eyes are almost colourless, this morning, making her face look even more striking.

'I'm deeply religious. I've always had a strong sense of inner peace, and I believe my faith plays a great part in that. My belief – in people's goodwill, in life and what the future holds – is unshakeable. Despite all that, I have encountered difficulties in my life that have been hard to overcome. It was a long time ago. The resulting depression caused my insomnia, and the only thing that brought me any relief was prayer. I believe wholeheartedly in the power of prayer. When my parish priest, who has since become a dear friend, learned about my sleep problems, he offered to give me a copy of the key to the church so that I could go there at night, safe from prying eyes.'

'Just to pray?' asks Lena.

'To pray, do a little cleaning, or handle administrative tasks for church. I like to feel useful.'

'But why alone? And why can't you do all that in the daytime? It would be more practical, don't you think?'

'There's something else, which will seem quite strange, or even crazy, to you, though I assure you it's not.' It's clearly hard for her to say it out loud. Plus we're all hanging on to every word, with bated breath, which probably doesn't help. 'I go to the church at night to . . . to talk to the children.'

I look around at the others, who seem as lost as I am.

'What children?' asks Lena. I'm relieved she's asked. No one else would have dared.

'Mine . . .'

Poor Lena goes even whiter than usual. We're all in a state of shock.

'Shit, that's awful,' she mumbles.

'No, sorry, don't misunderstand me. That's not what I meant. They're not dead! They were never born . . .'

Michèle laughs nervously. Jacques looks up at her with renewed interest, as he senses a potential new patient.

'Have you ever seen someone about this?' he asks.

'I'm not crazy, Jacques. I know they don't really exist. But I believe in angels.'

Hélène, quiet until now, feels she's losing her grip on the conversation and intervenes to regain control. 'Couldn't you pray from your bedroom? That way you could still follow your schedule.'

'It wouldn't be the same. We can only communicate by the grace of God. And His presence is most strongest in His house. And, it's so different . . . We can only speak in the dead of night.'

'What do you say to them?' asks Lena, who seems to have an endless list of questions.

'The sort of things people say to their children every day. No more, no less. I listen to their questions, try to answer them, reassure them. You know . . .'

'I think that's beautiful,' says Hervé, his voice hoarse from lack of use.

'Do you have any children, Hervé?' asks Michèle.

'A son, whom I see very little.'

'That's terrible! You must strengthen your relationship!'

'That's nuts . . . And do they answer?' Lena continues, ignoring Hervé. 'I mean, do you hear them?'

'Come now, Lena, give Michèle a little room. Let's have a look at your nights,' says Hélène, sounding more authoritative now.

I realise Hélène needs a way out. But if she's hoped to find it with Lena she'll be disappointed, as her results aren't any more promising than Michèle's. She still wakes up at exactly the same time every morning.

'You should come and pray with me,' jokes Michèle.

As for Hervé, Hélène congratulates him for stopping his afternoon naps at work, though it hasn't had any impact at all on his nights.

I discreetly study this man in his oversized trench coat. With his lost-boy allure, he inspires equal measures of pity and endearment. I'm willing to bet he never really had any friends at school, but somehow avoided becoming the class laughing-stock. The invisible, terribly middling student. And now he's the man who eats alone at his desk, or whom others invite to join them to cross off their good deed for the day. I'm certain he lives alone. And why is he always putting his hand over his heart like that? The hands on the large clock on the wall seem to be stuck. I sigh impatiently.

'Ah, Claire. It's your turn.'

I don't really feel like talking about myself, so I decide to lie, to shorten my torture. I tell her I followed all the rules but haven't noticed any improvements.

'The most important thing is to stick to your new schedules, your new bed- and wake-up times. And please don't forget to fill out your logs. We're done for today. Jacques, I'm sorry, we ran out of time, but I'll send you an email. And don't forget, everyone: keep hoping and believing, and you'll find your way back to normal sleep.'

I feel bad about lying. As for Jacques, he doesn't seem to mind that Hélène didn't get to him. No one moves. It's as if the exhaustion has worn us down a little more with each session, to the point where the very idea of braving the streets in broad daylight has become a terrifying prospect – one we try to put off as long as possible. Hervé, who usually rushes off at top speed so as not to be late, sips his tea. Lena, still huddled on her chair, nibbles a piece of cake. Jacques, who's clearly had a few too many sleeping pills, has gone back to sleep in the armchair. Hélène gathers our logs and jots down a few notes in her book. I still haven't left my seat.

'So, Michèle,' I venture, 'were you ever able to have children?'

She takes her time to answer. 'I became pregnant three times. I wanted them all so badly. Unfortunately, none of them made it to term.'

'Miscarriages?'

'People always make light of them, don't you think? They used to back then, anyway. It's so hard, though, the grief. The last one was the worst. It was a miracle when I became pregnant at the age of forty-five and at the end of the first trimester, I proudly told everyone who would listen. But three weeks later there were complications and the baby died. The shock and disbelief were unimaginable. That marked the beginning of a terrible depression and unbearable insomnia that I fought for five long years. Until, that is, my priest spoke to me outside church after mass one day: "Thinking of them will bring you peace someday, and they'll guide you like angels – you'll see." Those few words were like a revelation to me. I started going to church every day to commune with them. And then I started actually talking to them. I'd chosen their names in the first weeks of my pregnancies,' she explains, showing me her bracelets. 'But the prying looks became difficult to bear, so the priest said I could come at night, since I didn't sleep anyway. The only problem is that my nightly visits made me start sleeping even less. Do you have any children, Claire?'

'My husband does, yes. He has an eight-year-old son, but I . . .'

'Would you like to?'

'I . . . No, I think it scares me.' I'm always lost for words when asked that question.

Luckily, Hélène, who has been eavesdropping, cuts me off. 'That's a moving story, Michèle. Depression is one of the main causes of insomnia. What's interesting about your case is that it illustrates how insomnia can sometimes continue, even once the underlying cause has been identified and managed. Most of the time it settles in for the long haul. Nevertheless, I mean what I said. You'll never get back to normal sleep cycles if you keep going out at night. It'll take a while, but it will work if you stick with it. We'll talk about it again next time.'

Hélène puts her things away in her leather messenger bag and leaves.

'Why did you sign up for this?' I ask Michèle. 'It seems that not sleeping isn't really a problem for you. And you're retired, so it's not as if you have to get up in the mornings.'

She lets out a loud laugh. 'My doctor husband scared me to death with talk of a link with Alzheimer's! It was he who filled out the endless pages of questionnaires, though it was with my agreement, of course. I always wait until he's fallen asleep before going to the church. He doesn't approve,' she concludes, her expression darkening. Hervé, straightening his long legs as he stands, is the first among us to leave, waving shyly in my direction. Lena gets up in silence and begins wrapping the cake leftovers in some clingfilm she's brought from home, urging those of us still here to take a piece. She puts one at the foot of Jacques' chair, then heads off to her accounting class.

'I like that girl,' says Michèle as she watches her leave. 'I hope she makes it. I think she's struggling with her course.'

'Not surprising, considering she's only getting four hours' sleep per night,' I agree.

'Do you think I'm a dotty old lady?' Michèle asks out of the blue.

'Of course not,' I say.

Monday, 1.30 a.m. The phone rings, waking Jacques, who's been asleep for less than half an hour. He looks at the time on the ceiling. She had already called at midnight. He'd almost picked up the phone, too. With his new restricted sleep schedule, he's found himself waiting for her call rather than letting it wake him from his tormented sleep. 1.30 a.m. isn't her usual time. *Is she trying to wake him up?* he wonders. He gets up, but the phone stops ringing. What sort of game is she playing? Since he's up, he drags himself to his office wearing a worn, old dressing gown over his elegant flannel pyjamas. He sits down in his chair and turns on the Murano blown-glass desk lamp. The minimalist sphere on a brass base sheds a gentle light on the luxurious leather top of the antique desk – a perfect fit for the room, which is decorated in a warm, classical style. The phone rings again. Jacques hesitates, wondering if she's trying to send him a message. Curiosity – or perhaps it's irritation – eventually gets the better of him and he answers the phone.

'Marie?'

The breathing on the other end of the line is faint.

'Marie? Can you hear me?'

He picks up his Mont Blanc fountain pen out of habit – he always uses it to take notes about his patients' dreams during sessions – and starts doodling directly on the leather desk top, which has remained pristine for so many years.

'Has something happened, Marie?' he continues.

But she remains silent. He waits for a few minutes, to see

if she'll decide to talk. He presses down harder with the pen, leaving furrows in the leather.

'I'm going to hang up now,' Jacques warns. But before he has the chance, the continuous beeping tells him she's beaten him to it. He stays at his desk, lost in thought. He leans over the leather top and carefully blackens the entire surface.

4 a.m. When he's finished, he smiles, satisfied with the result. As he stands up he accidentally knocks over a cup of cold coffee from the day before, but heads back to his room without bothering to clean it up. He takes another half of a Noctamide and falls asleep, despite the feelings of worry he can't seem to shake off.

Tuesday, 1.00 a.m. Michèle is at the church again. The thought of going to bed and waiting to fall asleep has made her anxious, and the call of her children is still so strong. Her restricted sleep schedule has made things harder, though. She feels compelled to follow as much of Hélène's method as she can, so that she doesn't nap in the mornings anymore, which means she has to get by with an average of four hours' sleep.

She sits down on a pew at the far end of the nave and closes her eyes. Faint sounds break the magisterial silence, echoing off the stone walls. After a few minutes she can feel their presence and hear their voices. They become clearer, more real. Their new closeness fills her with joy.

The daytime candles are still burning, piercing the darkness with their weak flames. In the dim light Michèle notices the silhouette of a woman wrapped in a winter coat and wearing a thick woollen hat. The mysterious shadow moves slowly up the side aisle. Intrigued, Michèle gets up to follow her. The woman continues, unperturbed, lighting candles on her way.

When she's passed the choir, she sits down in front of a side chapel. Michèle stays two or three yards back.

'Hello,' she whispers, afraid she'll scare her away.

The woman turns around, stands up slowly, and nods in reply. She's young, and her face, which is hard to make out clearly in the darkness, is far from threatening. Nevertheless, Michèle can't help but shiver as the mysterious figure – who, she notices, is wearing fuchsia trainers – turns away from her and disappears. Disturbed by this unlikely encounter, Michèle sits back down on her pew – she'll have to ask the priest if any other parishioners have keys. She tries again, in vain, to reach out to her children, but they're gone. Something has come between them, and she can't even hear them now. They were so close just a few minutes ago. Deeply troubled, she prays earnestly.

6.00 a.m. The clicking of the fuse box followed by the lights coming on in the church wake her. Next comes the sound of creaking as the church caretaker opens the heavy doors to the street. Michèle can feel the urban bustle fill the previously calm space. It's morning. It takes her a few seconds to realise she's fallen asleep and her confusion worries her. That's never happened before. She stands up, massaging her sore muscles, and walks around the church. The woman is gone. She has to hurry home – if her husband wakes to an empty bed, he'll know she's been to the church and will threaten to have her put in a home again.

Wednesday, 5.30 a.m. She's been lying wide awake in bed for an hour. Getting up has become more and more difficult, but Lena refuses to waste the day. She gets dressed in the dark, then makes her way to the bathroom for her morning ritual. Mascara, then lipstick. She decides to try out a fancy hairdo with three French plaits joined together at the ends. She saw it on one of the rich New Yorker teens in *Gossip Girl*. Lena watches it non-stop, hypnotised by the luxurious homes, the beautiful girls who all get their first facelift before they have any wrinkles, the designer clothes – everything she dreams of having and being someday. The hairstyle turns out to be more complicated than she thought, and not really suited to her thin hair. She can't even imitate a rich girl's hairdo, she thinks in despair. Instead, she decides to go for a simple side plait and tiptoes out of the flat to avoid waking her mother.

6.30 a.m. Outside, the world has begun to turn again and the lost faces she usually sees in the morning blend into those of passers-by, then disappear completely. When she reaches the café, Franck is already serving the bin men who are joking loudly. A gold garland hangs from the bar, a small, blinking Christmas tree sits next to the radio, and baubles dangle from the ceiling. The early-morning workers quieten down to say good morning to Lena as she walks past, heading for the far end of the café, for a bit of peace and quiet. Franck looks at her curiously, his eyes asking, 'Since when do you turn up at this time?' She's feeling a little dizzy this morning, so she takes a croissant from the wicker basket and tries to choke a bite down, but she just can't manage it. Her meeting with the head of the department at college is at eight o'clock, before classes start and, given the way her head is spinning, she's afraid she might pass out on the Métro. Plus she knows all too well why the head has summoned her. Although it's supposedly a simple year-end review, Lena's no fool. She has failed her mock exams. Her marks arrived in the post, though she luckily managed to intercept them. She already knows the lecture she is going to get off by heart: *Lena, if you don't straighten yourself out, and quick, you won't get your diploma.*

But she's too tired to be angry this morning. Giving up suddenly seems so much easier than fighting what is clearly her destiny. She might as well go home and get back to bed. She'll tell her mother she's sick and spend the day in bed. Sleep.

She looks at the clock. François must be up already. She'd better get home to make him his hot chocolate.

Thursday, 11 p.m. The same questions have been running through Hervé's head for hours as he lies on his sofa. How did this happen? How did he accidentally erase weeks of work? Why didn't he keep a backup? He usually has at least three! What key could he have unwittingly pressed? He wonders if he lost consciousness for half a second. His mind was clouded this morning – his inability to concentrate has been getting more and more pronounced. And yet Hélène had said things would get better. He had thought he could count on his experience and expertise despite the overwhelming tiredness, but today's unforgivable mistake proved him wrong. His feet, hanging over the far end of the sofa, are exposed to the cold air, and he shivers under his blanket. He picks up his phone, then puts it down again, postponing the fateful moment when he'll finally have to check his emails. He hasn't dared to since coming home. His teeth are chattering, and he feels feverish. It's little things like this that can completely change the course of a life. A professional error is no crime, but it can transform an already difficult life into a living hell.

Hervé tries to calm down. He knows he's losing it. For the fifth time he picks up his phone in his clammy hands. This time he opens his email. He was expecting this, but his heart jumps into his throat anyway. His boss's name in bold at the top of the list. Hervé notices the message is short and decides that's a good sign. It ends with 'Thank you' so he works up the courage to read it. The tone is friendly, even relaxed. They're just asking him to stay late after work on Monday to go over a few figures. There's no mention of the table he lost during the annual meeting. In the advertising world staying 'a little late' means staying all night. He has no choice but to accept. So much for the food shopping he had planned to do for dinner with his son on Wednesday. He won't have enough time to cook properly either. You can't improvise Christmas dinner. He had worked out a two-day schedule in order to get everything ready on time.

Hervé rereads the email. Try as he might, he can't find a single reproach. But perhaps that's a bad sign. His heart begins to race as panic overwhelms him. His anxiety assails him with a slew of incoherent thoughts: the shopping he won't be able to do, the dinner menu he'll have to change, the worry about his meeting with his boss, the things he might say to defend himself. He must be careful now. If he loses his job, he'll have nothing left. He'll get unemployment benefit, but then what? Who will ever agree to hire someone like him? He'll have to move house, find something even smaller, if possible. But no one will want to rent a flat to a man without a job. Fear grips him like a vice. He sits up, places his computer on his lap and begins to check his bank accounts, going over his meagre savings as he estimates his spending, including child support, of course. The results are worrying. He won't last long. His world has turned upside down – tonight it's the figures that are running the show and the inescapable truth they spell out makes him feel small and insignificant. His stomach begins to cramp and his head hurts. *Breathe, just breathe.* He shakes his hands, desperately trying to ease the sensation of pins and needles. It takes every bit of energy he has to get up and go to the bathroom to splash cold water on his face.

1.30 a.m. He still doesn't feel great, but at least the attack is over. Despite his weakness and exhaustion, he wants to go out, to prevent it from happening again. But he needs to sleep. He must look rested at work tomorrow. If he turns up with huge circles under his eyes, they'll say his mistake was due to his lack of sleep. Alone in his pyjamas in the dark, surrounded by the sleeping city, Hervé clenches his jaw to hold back the tears of anguish he hasn't allowed to flow since his mother died.

Friday, 3.30 a.m. The very heart of a sleepless night. I eagerly await the dawn, but also fear it, for while it will mark the end of this period of torture, it will also signal the beginning of another. My mind wanders as I fall deeper into my nocturnal madness. Tonight, when she saw how bad I was looking, Françoise openly expressed her scepticism about the group sessions. I admitted I haven't been following the rules to the letter. 'Then why go?' she asked. It's true, what's the point? I then gave her some brief, but affectionate, descriptions of the other people in the group, and she seemed taken with them, agreeing that, all in all, they were probably a good reason for carrying on.

At this time of night, parties are still going strong in the city. The night owls who attend them aren't petrified by the countdown to morning, though. For them, staying awake is a choice, not a torment. Far from the lights and parties, I still can't sleep. The cold seems to seep through the walls, and I shiver under the covers.

Here we go again. I'm terrified the world is about to end, that a global disaster is imminent. The fear seems bottomless, inescapable. Death and disease stalk me from either side of my bed. Paul's presence used to soothe me. I try to remember the sense of peace I used to have at the beginning of our relationship, just knowing that he was sleeping next to me. What if I hadn't listened to him? What if I'd refused to move here, to the country, with him? I think of the lights on all night, of steps in the stairwell, of lives going on behind the windows of all the apartment buildings. What if we had stayed in the familiar bustle of the city?

I have to work this weekend. That thought keeps going round and round in my head, but it's not the most soothing of mantras. I'm falling so far behind that if I don't catch up now, I never will. The same goes for all those admin documents piling up on my desk that I still haven't got round to filling out. A bailiff will turn up at my door soon if I don't take care of them. Paul says I have administration phobia – a relatively common and potentially crippling disorder. I don't even bother suggesting that he might help me rather than just stand there watching me drown in paperwork. The fear that I'll be unable to meet the demands of tomorrow, unable to live up to the norms dictated by those lucky people who manage to get a good night's sleep, makes me want to cry. When people ask me why I don't use my nights more productively, I explain that I'm simply too tired. My brain is running on overdrive, but my body is limp. The only thing I can do is wait – for sleep or for sunrise. So I lie down and wait. Like a sailor's wife who won't leave her house for fear her long-lost husband might knock on her door one morning when she's not there.

4 a.m. I drag myself out of bed and stumble towards the bathroom. I plug in the hair dryer and move it in circles over my stomach and then the back of my neck. The warm air makes my body shiver pleasurably and finally relaxes my muscles. My breathing slows down, my eyelids feel heavy, my eyes close, and I fall blissfully to sleep. I'd be perfectly happy to spend the rest of the night sitting on the tiles with my back against the wall, but the door flies open.

'For Christ's sake, not the hair dryer!'

It's Paul in his boxers and T-shirt. I look up at him and, I'm not sure why, but the first thing that strikes me is how handsome he looks, standing there with his hair all tousled from bed. His colleagues at work must find him charming – I should probably appreciate him more. I explain, once again, how much better the hair dryer makes me feel.

'Take a sleeping pill!' he shouts.

I wonder if he regrets what he's just said. He should know better. No more sleeping pills for me. About two years ago I went a little overboard. It wasn't attempted suicide – I'm much too afraid of death to try to bring it on myself – but there was no explaining that to those around me, who saw me as a fragile little girl they needed to watch over constantly. I just wanted to sleep and had started to up my daily dose just to see what it felt like. And on that particular night I didn't count the pills. Or maybe I did, but didn't worry about the consequences. When I woke up in the hospital, Paul was there. I've never seen him so angry. 'Don't you ever do that to me again!' he screamed from the other side of the room. I was ashamed, like a child who suddenly realises that she's done something naughty. They weaned me off the pills after that, and I experienced the worst insomnia of my life. I'll never ever take a sleeping pill again, even though I'm desperate for one every night.

'Could you close the door now?' I ask, trying to sound polite, but despite all my efforts, my contempt shows through.

'Do whatever you want. I'm going to sleep in the guest room,' Paul replies with a sigh.

In the beginning he would hold the hair dryer over me himself, directing the warm air at my body, from my toes to the top of my head. Our relationship may have been based on a misunderstanding – and I prefer not to look too closely at our current feelings – but our first years together were certainly happy. There was so much affection between us. But that was before we moved here and my insomnia took over my nights, overwhelming me with the anxiety that frightens him so much. As if lack of sleep could drive me mad. I could do with a more reassuring partner. But I think the masks have fallen away now and my unhealthy need for praise and recognition, which pushed me into Paul's arms in the first place, has come back to haunt me. He's no longer the funny, charismatic, self-confident man who made me feel valued, but a domineering and inflexible bully whose only aim in life is to succeed – whatever the cost. For too long now, his view of me has made me feel small, has dragged me down deeper. But perhaps I drove him to it? I'm freezing, but I stay still, paralysed – no longer by doubts, but by the panic I feel at the obvious state of my marriage.

He'll never accept a second failed relationship; he'd rather continue as we are than do that. But I know that if I don't free myself from him, his indifference and my weakness for failure will be the end of me.

5

Monday, 8.10 a.m. Strands of Christmas lights decorate our attic room. I pause in the doorway, surveying the scene. Lena, still perched on a ladder, is just finishing her handiwork. Michèle is slowly cutting up a star-shaped cake. Jacques holds his head in his hands, mumbling incomprehensibly, while Hervé is staring blankly into space from behind his glasses, which are sitting askew on his nose. All in all, the group isn't looking too great.

'That's better, isn't it?' asks Lena, looking satisfied as she walks towards us.

I tell her it feels like Disneyland.

'I can never tell if you're being serious or not,' she replies.

I can see she's looking a bit uncertain and assure her that I love Christmas decorations, and always have done, ever since I was little. Lena relaxes and proudly admires her work. We've all finished our first cup of coffee when a woman in a white coat comes in to tell us Hélène won't be able to attend today's meeting because of an emergency. She asks us to leave our sleep logs on the table. Jacques immediately flops down into his armchair.

'A pity. I would have liked to talk to her about the nightmares I've been having,' says Michèle.

'We can all listen, Michèle,' says Hervé. 'I have to spend tonight at the agency, so I'm in no hurry to get there this morning.'

'And my college isn't open yet,' adds Lena.

I like Hervé's idea – and I certainly have no desire to turn around and go home. Michèle tells us about the hell her nights have become. As soon as she falls asleep she wakes up terrified, but unable to remember the dream that has put her in such a state and left her body so paralysed with fear. And it takes her quite a while to get over it.

'These are night terrors, not nightmares. Dreams only happen later, during REM sleep,' explains Jacques from his armchair.

'Is that supposed to reassure Michèle, doctor?' I ask from across the room.

'Accurate and rational explanations are often reassuring,' he replies with a long sigh that underscores the obvious nature of his observation.

'I think Hélène would say everything would go back to normal if she followed the guidelines. Like not going to church at night,' I venture.

Michèle looks down at her feet. I immediately regret making her feel bad and apologise. There is something about Jacques's authoritative tone that has got under my skin and made me lash out.

Michèle admits that she goes back every night, thus betraying both Hélène's trust in her and her husband. He doesn't want to know about her 'mystical outings', as he calls them. He accepted them at first, as they were the only thing that seemed to ease her depression, but only on condition that she didn't talk about it at home or with anyone else. He's a pious man, she says, but perhaps the pain of never experiencing the joys of fatherhood has made him intransigent.

'It's a shame,' I say, 'to have to hide your fears from your partner in life.'

'There's nothing that says you have to share the worst things,' replies Jacques.

'No, but the most intimate things, at least,' I contend.

Hervé keeps his mouth shut. The topic seems to make him uncomfortable. Lena adds that she won't even consider spending her life with someone else. It didn't work out that well for her parents. Then again, maybe she'll try it, but there'll be no promises of fidelity. Her father left two years ago, she says. He went back home, to Algeria, with a customer he became infatuated with. Overnight he decided to close his bakery and leave his family. Ever since she was a child she had woken up every day at 4.30 a.m., the time when he got up for work. She liked to listen as he got everything ready – she found it re-assuring – and as soon as he closed the door behind him, she would go back to sleep. But since he has left for good, some-thing inside her forces her to stay awake. She's spinning a strand of hair in circles with her knees hugged close to her chest.

'You're still so young,' says Michèle. 'You'll change your mind, you'll see. Some day you'll meet the man of your dreams.'

'Man of my dreams, what nonsense. Times have changed,' Lena replies caustically. 'There are no more prince charmings. Maybe a child, but no husband. No thank you.'

I serve myself another piece of cake. This girl is becoming terribly endearing.

'What about you, Claire?' ask Michèle. 'Would you like to have children? You didn't get a chance to answer properly last time.'

'No . . . It's not part of my plans, anyway.'

'Really?' says Lena. 'I know you sometimes act like you couldn't give a damn about things, but I reckon that, deep down inside, there's a really motherly side to you.'

'You're right!' adds Michèle.

'I don't think so,' I reply coldly, keen to put a stop to the discussion. 'I'm not strong enough for that kind of respon-sibility. I'm too angry. I'm always about to explode, so can you imagine what I would be like with a child? I'm not even sure I'd know how to love him or her.'

'Don't be silly,' exclaims Michèle with a chuckle.

Maybe she's right, I think to myself, but I remember that one of the first things that came to mind when I met Paul was, oh, thank goodness, he already has one. I'm off the hook. My mother, who equates monogamy with having children – once you've got at least one advanced degree in hand, of course – has never forgiven me for my decision. Her only daughter has deprived her of the joys of being a grandmother. She's never been able to move on. I can't help but see how preposterous it is for a woman who never knew how to take care of her own child to tell me that a woman without children is a failure. Or did I imagine that conversation, like the stars in my childhood bedroom? One night when I was eavesdropping from the top of the stairs, I heard her tell my father, 'If I hadn't been pregnant, I would have got that job in London.' She sounded bitter. I couldn't hear my soft-spoken father's reply.

The thing I've never told my mother, or any other mother, is the way I really see women like them. How respectful and humble they make me feel as they bravely push their buggies through the streets. Their pale faces convey something indescribable, somewhere between exhaustion, distress and pride. Warriors. Superheroes. They know what's what. They have carried life in their wombs. And now, whatever the cost, they'll watch over their babies every night and protect them from the slightest danger. I'm secretly jealous because I could never live up to that role.

I turn to Hervé. His eyes are closed, his hand over his heart. He nearly jumps out of his skin when I ask him why he's always doing that.

'My mother. She spent her whole life placing her hand on my heart, like this,' he explains, doing it again.

I stare in disbelief. What a strange man.

'She was terrified that my heart might stop.'

'Why?'

'I had a heart attack at the age of three, in the middle of the night.'

'That can happen at three?' asks Lena, surprised.

'Not usually, no. I'm a medical phenomenon. My mother only just managed to save me. Her instincts brought her to my room just as my heart stopped. After that, she was so afraid it would happen again that she did everything she could to keep me from sleeping. She would read me stories until it was late, then come into my room ten times a night to make sure I was still breathing. When I got too old for that, she got me hooked on TV shows, which I would watch until the ridiculously early hours of the morning. She died when my son was ten years old.'

'And there was no one to keep you awake at night. Or make sure your heart was still working. So your unconscious took over,' concludes Michèle.

'Something like that.'

'We all know a hand over a heart has never prevented a heart attack, right?' I ask.

Hervé looks at me, perplexed, as if trying to solve a mystery.

It's nearly nine o'clock. Hélène turns up, apologising profusely. She's surprised we're all still here. She just came to get our sleep logs, but she takes advantage of the opportunity to wish us all a Merry Christmas.

I remain in my seat, completely depressed . . . Christmas.

Thursday, 3.27 a.m. This is the third time he's woken up since going to bed at midnight on the dot, surprised to find himself following the rules so scrupulously. The telephone didn't ring. Strange. A Christmas truce, perhaps? Jacques turns on his new bedside lamp, bought in the sale from Ikea, and shivers from the cold as he stands up. In the bathroom, without so much as a glance at his puffy face, he tries in vain to open the medicine cabinet. Something's stuck. He takes a deep breath, sighs, mumbles, then very calmly makes his way towards the other end of the flat and comes back with a rarely used toolbox. He uses a screwdriver to carefully remove the hinges and, once he's finished, he puts the right-hand cabinet door on the floor then does the same thing with the left-hand door, even though it's pointless. He stares at the near-naked shelves, hesitating between several tidily arranged boxes, but eventually opts for the Rohypnol, which he generally reserves for special occasions – in other words, totally sleepless nights. He can already feel tonight will be one. He decides not to worry about the Stilnox he took a few hours ago. It won't kill him – hell, he might even sleep. He goes back to bed, slightly soothed by the idea that the pharmaceuticals will help him nod off. He doesn't even bother to pick up his mess.

He lies in bed, watching the red numbers projected on the ceiling tick past as he waits for the medicine to kick in and starts thinking about tomorrow. His wife is set to arrive early in the morning. She's returning from a two-month trip to India, where she completed a massage or yoga training course (he can't quite remember which but it was some sort of silent retreat). His daughter, who's studying at a prestigious art school in Tokyo, will be home for lunch. And then there are his two sons, who are complete opposites. One of them lives in a yurt in Auvergne with his partner, who's expecting their first child. He can't bear to think about the child's living conditions. The other works in finance in New York, handling such astronomical sums that he could afford at least three flats like this one, in addition to several country homes. Jacques is looking forward to seeing all three of them. It'll be nice to have a family again just like old times. For a few days there will be discussions, arguments, appeals for advice, which he'll be happy to provide. He'll get back into his role as the man of the house, ruling the roost with brio. As a husband, however, he has zero expectations. Catherine will sleep in their bed, but he won't dare move close to her, much less touch her.

The knot in his stomach. The fear that he won't fall asleep, that he won't be able to stand up straight tomorrow, returns. He's always lived up to his role, regardless of the circumstances. Why didn't any of his children stay close to home? Were they unconsciously – or, worse, voluntarily – trying to escape him? He's certain he's been an excellent father. But what values did he really teach them? And when he talks about home, what exactly does he mean? His wife's rarely here now. Can he constitute a home all on his own? No one seems to want to spend any time here anymore.

These unanswered questions depress him and override the effect of the drugs. At five o'clock, still committed to following Hélène's guidelines as best he can, he gets up and makes himself a cup of tea. Despite his aching joints, he manages to drag his huge body to the kitchen and sits down at the large Scandinavian-style wooden dining table. An invisible hammer pounds relentlessly against his skull, as it always does after a sleepless night. His vision is still blurred by the sleeping pill he took too late, and his brain is slow. Given the way he's feeling, the family celebration, which should have been a pleasure, is now looking more like a nightmare. He's obsessed with finding the time for a nap, to rest a little before lunch. It's all he can think about.

Thursday, 12.00 a.m. Mass has just ended and Michèle watches the parishioners calmly leave the church as the choir sings one last hymn. The priest makes his way over to her.

'Merry Christmas, Michèle. Don't stay too late tonight,'

he says. He hesitates at the thought of leaving her. He's been worried about her for some time. She is always very uncomplaining, but he can tell she's exhausted. He hopes he didn't make a terrible mistake by encouraging her to come to the church at night. It had been helpful when she was suffering from depression years ago, but now he's not so sure. Michèle reassures him that she's fine. 'There's no need to worry,' she says, sending him on his way.

The church is quiet and dark once again – the way Michèle likes it. The many candles lit by the parishioners still burn throughout the sanctuary, making the shadows from the statues dance on the stone floor. She lights three more, then sits down near the altar.

Antoine, Paula, stop messing around, it's time to sleep now! No, Father Christmas isn't an angel. Dad will be there, I promise. Of course he lives here, what a silly question. We'll all have a lovely day together. OK, good night, I don't want to hear from you again until morning. Yes, I promise the night won't last for the whole of eternity, just long enough for you to recharge your batteries. I'm closing the door this time. Don't try calling me up here again. Good night, my darlings.

Michèle stands up. Her eyes are glassy, and a drop of sweat has pearled at her temple. She has to get home earlier tonight, or she won't make it through tomorrow. She slowly makes her way to the door, blowing out the candles and taking a moment to contemplate the church. She notices the woman in pink trainers standing by the choir. She's not alone this time. Someone is next to her, kneeling in prayer. Michèle shivers. Something's not right, but she can't put her finger on it. After all, the Lord is entitled to whichever nocturnal worshippers he wants.

Out in the street, her head down and coat collar up to keep out the cold, she quickens her step.

Alexandre, can we talk? Will you come and help me wrap the presents? I'm worried about you. You haven't said much at all lately. I may wear a cross around my neck, but you can still tell me everything, you know. I just wanted to make sure you knew that.

It's after two o'clock when Michèle tiptoes into her bedroom. 'Merry Christmas, Jean-Louis,' she whispers. But her husband is fast asleep. She usually falls asleep straight away after visiting the church, but not tonight. She feels strangely agitated. It was different this time. The children's voices seemed so real she thought they might actually appear before her. Yes, that's it – it was as if their voices had escaped the realm of the imaginary world and joined the real one.

I might need to mention this to the group, she thinks. Her eyes are wide open. The room seems darker than usual, and she covers her husband's hand with her own, trying to soothe herself. Just as she's about to drift off, a distant memory surfaces. She was eighteen years old and had been attending a religious retreat that was proving to be difficult: the monastery and surrounding countryside were terribly bleak; it was damp and she was always cold; silence was the rule. And on top of everything else, she was sleeping very badly. After dinner and the final group prayer of the day, she would return to her room – or rather her cell – with a rock in her stomach. After the first three bad nights, she had become more and more apprehensive and on the fourth night, she sat huddled on her bed with her knees pulled close to her chest and asked God for help. As she prayed, an icy wind threw open the window and, just as she was closing it, the door to her room burst open as well, as if someone had pushed it as hard as they could. Without thinking, she ran out into the corridor but no one was there. It was dark and she was terrified. Just then, drawn by the noise, a girl from the room next door came out in her long nightdress and moved towards Michèle, who turned pale. The girl's face was oddly white, and her eyes seemed to have no pupils. Michèle screamed as loud as she could, pointing her finger at the threatening apparition. 'It's the devil! The devil!' she kept screaming. A priest arrived at a run, turned on the lights and tried to calm her down. 'It's just a nightmare. Look, it's OK !' he reassured her. Michèle looked at the poor girl, who looked completely normal again. A waking nightmare. No one ever mentioned the episode afterwards, but it took Michèle several years to get over the terrifying experience.

Thursday, 5.35 a.m. Lena has been working in the kitchen for an hour. Nothing can bring her down on Christmas Day. Not her school troubles, nor her mother, nor her frustrations, nor even her stomach, which has stoically accepted a third cup of coffee without any food. Her exhaustion and her father's absence are nothing but distant clouds in her bright blue sky. This is her third Christmas without him. She had asked him to come and see them, but he explained that he couldn't leave his bakery without a replacement baker at this time of year. And then there was the price of the tickets . . . She let it go and is now focusing her attention on the puff pastry that she's nimbly shaping into crescents before placing them on the baking tray and popping them into the warm oven. Just seconds later, the smell of croissants fills the whole flat. Her brother rushes into the kitchen, jumping up and down.

'François, what are you doing here? Go back to bed!'

Wearing Spiderman pyjamas, the curly-haired little boy comes to stand right next to his big sister and has a go at shaping the pastries, turning them into strange zigzags. Lena lets her brother get on with it and, with a look of disgust, turns her attention to the turkey – a huge slab of pink meat.

'Why don't you ask ask Mum to help you?' suggests François.

'No need to bother her.'

'You think the two of us can eat all that?' he asks.

'We'll soon find out!' Lena replies cheerfully.

Their conversation is interrupted by the doorbell. The early morning caller, whoever it is, is insistent, and the bell continues to ring as Lena hurriedly washes her hands. Before leaving the kitchen she tousles her brother's dark curly hair and he squeals with joy.

'Oh, hi, Franck. What are you doing here?' asks Lena.

'I'm not opening the café today, and I thought maybe you could use a hand.'

François jumps down to welcome Franck.

'Hey Superman!' he says to the boy. Then he turns to Lena. 'What a mess! How were you planning to stuff the turkey?'

'With my hands, like a big girl,' Lena replies, indignant.

'Where's your mother?'

'Where do you think? In her bedroom as usual, passed out from her pills.'

'I'll take care of the bird. Go and put this on,' he says, handing her a broken plastic CD case.

'Christmas songs? Is this yours?' she asks in surprise.

'Do you want to do this properly or not?' he asks earnestly.

'At least François will enjoy it.'

In the kitchen, where the work surface is now completely covered in utensils and ingredients, Lena and Franck prepare a proper Christmas feast while François drinks his hot chocolate and sings 'Jingle Bells'.

'Franck, do you want to hear something funny? One of the people in my insomniacs group is a psychiatrist who takes fistfuls of sleeping pills! Isn't that the pot calling the kettle black?'

He laughs, then asks, 'Hey, how did your mock exams go?'
'Great,' she replies evasively.

Friday, 12.10 a.m. The plates of food are left half-eaten on
the table. Turkey with mushroom gravy, vegetable gratin and
roasted potatoes. The centre of the Yule log is a fruity mousse,
to keep the dessert light. The menu would have been more
elegant if Hervé had had time to cook as he'd planned. He
left the agency after midnight yesterday, under orders to take
a week's holiday. Despite his protests, his boss was unyielding.
Hervé dreads holidays more than anything else and takes as
little time off as possible. When he has no choice but to stay
at home, he spends his days sleeping, unable to work up the
strength to go food shopping or make a proper meal. He
survives on a diet of pasta, cereals and biscuits, and barely
showers. The TV is always on. He lets himself go completely.
He's ashamed but can't resist the urge to vegetate. So that's
what he'll be doing from tomorrow onwards. Thank goodness
dinner is over.

His son had arrived early for their meal and brought a
present – the latest bestseller on the economic crisis. Hervé
had prepared an envelope of cash for him. He noticed his
son's embarrassment when he came into the flat – obviously
a bit of a shock for someone who lives in a trendy loft. Hervé
felt pathetic.

He sits down and serves himself a piece of cake, going
back over their vain attempts to behave as if they had a close
father–son relationship. Yet again he regrets how things went.
Every year he vows to try to forge real ties with his son. He
even practises potential topics for discussion in advance, as
if preparing for a role in a play. He needs to learn to talk
about something other than his job, which doesn't interest
anyone at all.

There are so many topics to choose from. But Hervé can't even manage to bring up his insomnia, which embarrasses him. He could tell his son that it was after his mother died that it all started, the not sleeping. That's when it all fell apart, when family life became impossible. Countless sleepless nights, sleeping pills, antidepressants. He had to leave – he didn't even try to fix things. His son was only ten then. Hervé serves himself a glass of champagne. What a disaster. The conversation was slow, shallow and boring. His son had left before the dessert – disappointed as well, no doubt, and on his way out had said a terrible thing: 'Dad, let me know if you need anything . . .' Hervé mumbled a 'thank you'. The shame was suffocating. When the door closed again, he noticed the envelope he'd given his son, left forgotten on the hallway table.

He doesn't have the strength to clean up, but knows another radio show will finish him off, so he paces the flat like a caged animal. He puts the envelope in a drawer, mentally adding the amount to his next child support payment, then puts on his coat.

1.00 a.m. Happily, his café is open – a haven for the lost and lonely on Christmas night. The tables are mostly empty, but a few regulars are sitting at the bar drinking the night away. The owner, who seems to be in a good mood, is offering rounds on the house. As soon as Hervé walks in, a tall brunette in an unseasonably scanty outfit places herself right across from him, far too close for any semblance of propriety.

He attempts to escape politely to his table, but she doesn't seem inclined to let him out of her grip this time. She's older than she looks. Her breath smells of alcohol and her pores are clearly visible. The huge circles under her eyes show through a thick layer of make-up. All her efforts to look young have been in vain. Her slightly swollen eyes shine like her sequinned dress and greasy hair. Hervé feels sorry for her but does his best to be convincing as he explains that he needs to be alone, that he's had a bad night. She doesn't move.

Exhausted, he gives in. There's no point, she won't budge. Maybe he doesn't really want her to, after all. What does it matter? After that disastrous dinner, all he would do if he were on his own is just go over things again.

She brings him over to the bar, where they welcome him with a 'Hurrah' and a toast. Without really joining the group, Hervé finds a place for himself among the regulars, who are all at least a head shorter than him. He drinks more than usual, which gets him talking. He tells them how little he sleeps, explains that's why he comes here. Everyone seems delighted to finally hear his voice.

4 a.m. Hervé leaves on the arm of the sequin-clad woman, stumbling in the freezing cold, to end his sleepless night. A few minutes later, sitting on the bed in a clinical-looking studio with soulless contemporary furniture, he watches her take her clothes off. She feigns sensuality, as if imitating a trashy TV show she's watched again and again. In the half-light, she slowly reveals her plump, tired body. Her breasts surprise him – they must have had some sort of special treatment to stay so high and firm above such a flaccid stomach. But her body moves him. When she comes over and kneels before him, he follows his natural instinct to caress her long, dyed, red hair. He's afraid he'll seem awkward or, worse still, indifferent. He wants to make her happy but doesn't quite know how. He'd like to be good at something for once on this Christmas night.

Thursday, 12.05 a.m. I make a list of the last few things I need to get done for tomorrow's festivities. Prepare lunch for my in-laws, set and decorate the table, wrap Thomas's presents, wash my hair, pluck my eyebrows, try to look as put-together as my mother-in-law, who is as charming and smart as her son and makes me feel just as bad about myself.

1.20 a.m. The problem is that my body and my brain are incapable of producing the energy I need to accomplish these simple tasks. I won't be able to laugh, eat or hold up my end of a conversation. I won't be able to fake it. Paul will put his hand – the one that he pulls away every night – on mine. He'll pretend to be the perfect husband for his parents. He has to uphold his image, whatever the cost. I'll even get phoney loving glances. I can't bear the thought of it.

I try to remember the last time I slept normally. Fortunately, it does happen from time to time – when my body can't take it anymore, I suppose – but it's increasingly rare. And the group sessions aren't helping at all. I should have done the vegetables today and set the table. That would have saved me precious time tomorrow. Why didn't it occur to me earlier? I could go downstairs and do it now. No, I don't have the strength.

I watch the hours tick past without even trying to fall asleep. Then I wake up with a start, short of breath, and realise I must have been asleep after all. A nightmare. The same dark house, completely lacking in light. It takes me a few minutes to calm down enough to move my limbs. In dire need of physical contact, I touch Paul's hand – but he instinctively pulls away. His violent reaction leaves me paralysed again. The anxiety makes me nauseous. To escape his rejection, I get up and go to Thomas's room, where I find him fast asleep. His eyelids tremble slightly and sweat has glued his hair to his forehead. Is he dreaming? I lie down next to him. Thanks to the glow of the nightlight, the bedtime storybook on the nightstand, and toys scattered across the floor, this room is the only one in the house that soothes me. I stroke his hair. What is it that binds us so? The alarm clock reads 4.30 a.m. The first train leaves at five o'clock. I carefully extricate myself from the bed.

'Where are you going?' asks Thomas, stirring slowly.

'Out for a bit. Tell your father not to worry, OK?'

'OK. See you later,' he says sleepily.

'See you later, sweetheart.'

I grab yesterday's clothes off the floor and dress mindlessly. Downstairs, I quickly wrap Thomas's presents and place them under the magnificent tree dominating the lounge. Then I silently leave the house, on an impulse. It feels like a survival instinct, like raising your hands to protect your face from a threat. I have to spend today far away from here. I'll find an excuse. There was some last-minute shopping to do, and then Françoise called and told me she needed me. And I couldn't let my best friend down at Christmas, after all, could I? There will be a big fight when I come home, but that's better than the hell I'll have to endure if I stay. I've been so close to the limit of what I can handle for too long now and I know that if I don't take this train, I'll go beyond the point of endurance forever. So, what now? Getting to the city is the only thing I can think of.

It's totally dark outside – the village streetlights and decorations haven't been turned on yet. There's no one on the platform at the station. Carried by the wind, the roar of the train reaches me before the safety barriers come down and the bell sounds. I find a seat in the last carriage and look out of the window. I've taken apart and analysed this trip so many times, but, there's still always something new to admire.

The first three stations on the way to the city are still in the middle of nowhere. At this early morning hour in winter, the countryside is an impenetrable mass of darkness. But in warmer weather, or later in the summer, my eyes devour these landscapes. The first rays of sunshine cutting a path across the black tree trunks, a layer of white fog on a lake or marsh, with the occasional heron perched majestically on a promontory or a branch. At times like this, I feel as if I'm part of a mystical landscape, where shadows from another world might appear at any moment. As the day dawns, the countryside casts off the gloom of night to reveal its striking beauty. I've often asked myself whether chronic exhaustion can enhance the senses. When I glance around the carriage at the passengers' eyes focused on newspaper headlines, mobile screens or some cheap thriller, I wonder how those things can possibly win out over the living marvels on the other side of the glass. This morning I'm not even thinking about running away. The course of my life has escaped me – I'm no longer calling the shots.

After two or three minutes contemplating vast intensively cultivated fields, my eyes are suddenly confronted with concrete: the station at N. This is where the second half of the journey – much less rural but just as captivating – begins. An endless sprawl of incoherent and anxiety-provoking residential areas filled with mismatched yet strangely similar houses, some boasting tacky, ostentatious architecture, others struggling to stand under caving roofs and cracked walls. But they all have one thing in common: dull facades in unidentifiable shades. Whether carefully tended or abandoned, their gardens generate feelings of boredom and despair. Despite the speed of the train, I try to imagine myself inside one of these uniformly dull homes. Most of the time they're lit by neon lights or glaring ceiling fixtures. Screens too big for the rooms that house them are already on in many of the lounges.

But what surprises me most at this time of year is the way all the tiny gardens, so close to one another and attached to dilapidated houses, shine bright with Christmas lights. The residents' eagerness to participate in the year-end festivities is apparently undimmed by poverty. It's like a beacon of hope, a sign that they won't give up.

When the train pulls into A. station, the seemingly infinite suburbia suddenly disappears. What comes next is no better. Towering apartment buildings. The area I've just passed sprawled horizontally across the ground, while this one climbs threateningly towards the sky. Council estates that flaunt the inhumanity of their designers and provoke useless rage in me. Here too, I seek out bedrooms, lounges and kitchens, which are all considerably smaller than in suburbia, but unfortunately, the size of the windows in the train thwarts my curiosity. I imagine myself on the other side, behind one of the tiny windows, watching the early-morning trains and the other buildings, which block my view of the horizon, preventing all attempts at escape. A woman gets on the train and sits down a row away, facing me. She keeps her eyes closed, so I can watch her unhindered. She's wearing a pair of jeans under a long tunic covered in golden embroidery and a red silk headscarf covers her hair. Her cheeks are plump and soft, as is the rest of her body. Warm, spicy smells emanate from a large canvas bag sitting next to her. I can't look away. Strangely, this woman reminds me of the mother I imagined every night, lying in my childhood bed. In fact, the dreams continued until I was much older. I would lay my head on her lap and she'd stroke my hair slowly, humming a lullaby from some faraway land. Cuddled up against her maternal body, I would finally fall asleep. She was the universal archetype of motherhood.

Factories with smoking chimneys provide the final element of this urban landscape – an industrial touch that I find strangely beautiful – especially in the light of the rising sun. And finally comes the last and shortest part of the journey: the heart of the city with its squares and affluent neighbourhoods. The train slows down. The woman stands up.

I must speak to her. I can't stop myself. I can't let my imaginary mother get away, not at Christmas. Standing behind her at the doors, which are still closed, I compliment her on the delicious smells coming out of her bag. 'It's a tajine, my secret recipe. I'm on my way to spend Christmas at my daughter-in-law's house. I have to take two more trains!' she explains. I'm relieved when I hear the affectionate tone of her voice. She's not afraid of me. And her sing-song accent, it's just as I imagined it. Before stepping out onto the platform, she turns back towards me. 'You're not alone today, are you, sweetheart? You can't spend Christmas alone.' I reassure her with tales of a family waiting for me, just managing to stop myself from jumping into her arms and begging her to take me with her. I'm certain she would have done it.

The train station is quiet. There will be no rush hour today. I step out of the train full of determination; I can already feel the first inklings of relief. Today I won't have to please anyone but myself. Paul's family will feel sorry for him and won't have to hold back their criticism of me. He'll play the victim and come out on top. But now I wonder what I'll do with all this time. Wandering the streets feels too much like a punishment – I'm barely strong enough to take three steps. I could sit down in a café, but it will be a long day. A cinema, maybe? Too early . . . I hesitate for a few more minutes, then decide to walk into the first hotel I find that's close to the station. It's pretty shabby-looking, but cheap and I pay for the night upfront. The corridor leading to my room on the top floor has greying tiles that must once have been white. In the tiny, green-carpeted room my exhaustion finally gets the better of me. I lie down fully dressed on the synthetic pink bedcover and fall asleep instantly. A 'Get out of here, asshole!' followed by a slew of insults in return wakes me up. I look at my phone. It's nearly eleven o'clock at night. I've slept all day. I smile. I haven't slept that many hours in a row for years. I have ten messages from Paul, which I decide not to listen to. I send him a reassuring text message so he'll leave me alone.

Hunger and the seediness of the hotel convince me to go out. In the lobby, the receptionist stares insistently. He must wonder how a middle-class lady like me ended up in his establishment – and without so much as a suitcase.

I wander the streets for a long time looking for a café that's open on Christmas night. Nearly frozen to death, I finally find a humble but charming bistro. I order a bowl of soup and some mulled wine. No one seems to find it strange that I'm dining alone on this special night. The wine quickly goes to my head and it takes me a while to realise that my phone is ringing. I assume it's Paul yet again, or, worse still, my mother-in-law, but it's just a worried Françoise.

'What the hell are you doing, Goddammit?'

Françoise loves to swear. It's been her chosen form of rebellion against the wealthy, ultra-conservative milieu she was born into. She's been trying to escape it ever since the age of ten, when she realised exactly how privileged she was. Paul must have called her, assuming I was with her. She yells at me for not giving her a heads up – she had to improvise to cover for me. I change the subject, asking about her Christmas dinner, which is almost always a disaster. Françoise has chosen not to have children, and at every family get-together they rake her over the coals for it. She's not part of my plan. I could have told her all about it of course, but I don't want to do it tonight. She seems to understand.

'All right, then. So, see you Thursday? We have that concert. Don't forget, OK? It'll do you good.'

It's Francoise who taught me to love music, who showed me how to truly listen, beyond the emotions and images it stirs up. Thanks to her I've learnt about all sorts of things like timbres, melodies and tonality.

In the middle of a concert, she'll quietly explain, 'Did you hear that shift from major to minor key? Listen closely.' I don't know exactly what she means since I'm a complete neophyte, but I do as she says and begin to believe I can hear what she means. I trust her judgement and always let her choose the concert. She knows that I draw the line at Wagner. A night at one of his operas almost drove me crazier than my insomnia once.

'All right, well, don't worry about a thing. It will all turn out OK.' It's extraordinary how a few simple words said calmly by someone you love can be so unimaginably soothing.

I look towards the bar, blinking repeatedly. Maybe it's the alcohol, but I think I can see a man who looks exactly like Hervé, though his relaxed manner – nothing like what I've seen at our sessions – makes me doubt myself. When I watch him leave on the arm of a woman who is most definitely a prostitute, I tell myself I must be wrong.

It's getting late. The question is: do I take the first train home or opt for another night at the hotel?

I head towards the train station with a knot in the pit of my stomach, like a little girl who knows she's going to get an earful when she gets home.

6

Monday, 8.05 a.m. This morning, at our first meeting of the New Year, I readily admit we all look like zombies. Those pale faces and slumped bodies aren't fooling anyone – the Christmas season has left its mark. Michèle drinks her tea with her eyes closed. Hervé sits there in his oversized trench coat, his head drooping over his briefcase, much as on the first day. Lena's so skinny she would disappear if it weren't for the bright red lips signalling her presence. Jacques is fast asleep in the armchair. We wait silently for Hélène. The only sound in the room is the rapping of the rain on the attic window.

'Happy New Year, everyone!' says Hélène, softly, as she strolls in.

We all jump despite her soothing tone. Without so much as a glance at our defeated faces, she takes pens and notebooks out of her bag.

'Wake up, Jacques!' she scolds.

Jacques opens his eyes and drags himself over to the table to join us.

'You could let him sleep for once,' grumbles Lena.

'You're here to learn to sleep at night, Lena,' replies Hélène, emphasising the word 'night'.

'It doesn't look like your method is working for any of us,' I say.

'I was going to get to that, Claire. It's true you all look very tired. You've been applying the sleep restriction method for three months now. It's time to assess your progress and adapt your hours depending on how things are going.'

We hold out our logs, which tell the tale of our nights since the last meeting. As usual, only Hervé's and Michèle's are legible. I'm still as disgusted as ever by the exercise. I usually fill it in at the last minute, in the train, when I'm half asleep. And I still don't understand how the formulaic boxes in the logs can ever hope to convey the infinite yet infinitesimal details of our nights.

'Claire, haven't you slept more than two hours in a row since last time?' asks Hélène, surprised. 'Have you been following my instructions?'

'To the letter, I promise.'

My head feels heavy. I grab the thermos of coffee, which has replaced tea due to popular demand, and fill my cup to the brim. I start losing concentration as Hélène starts talking to Hervé about his log, her comments sounding very distant. The conversation slips away from me, but I quickly pick up the thread again when I hear Hervé's weak and trembling voice.

'I've been sacked. I got a letter during a week of mandatory leave,' he mumbles.

The room goes quiet. People don't fire discreet and gentle accountants like Hervé.

'Bastards. I thought they even let you nap in your fantastic ad agency,' exclaims Lena.

'As long as I performed as expected, yes. But when I stopped napping, I started falling asleep at my desk and my productivity plummeted. And then I made the ultimate mistake.'

'I'm so sorry, Hervé. That's so unfair. What will you do now?' Michèle asks compassionately.

'Sign up for unemployment benefits and look for a job. How are your twins, by the way?'

'All right, thanks,' replies Michèle.

'Good luck with the unemployment office. My mum's been out of work for years and they're not much help,' adds Lena, dejectedly.

I'm surprised by Michèle's evasive reply. She's usually very forthcoming on the subject of her children – her eyes light up and her voice fills with joy whenever she mentions Antoine, Paula and her eldest, Alexandre.

I'd like to join in, but I'm just too tired. I always come back to the same eternal, unanswerable question: how is it that I'm so exhausted all day, but unable to sleep at night? What, for most people on earth, is the most natural thing in the world is a nightly torture for all of us sitting around this table. As I contemplate the palm tree poster with its deep blue sea, my eyes close and I doze off, rocked by the rhythm of Hélène's speech in the background. I latch on to certain words to keep my head above water. Circadian rhythm, internal clock, experiments in caves, the din of several people talking at once, a rhythm incompatible with social life . . .

'I'd be happy to go and live in a cave, as long as I didn't ever have to come out,' says Hervé, interrupting the monotonous litany.

I pull myself out of the sea and turn to look at him. He's bright red. After a few seconds of silence – due to surprise, no doubt – everyone starts to chip in with their own comments about the disadvantages he would surely encounter living in a cave, though they agree the life of a recluse does seem ideal at first glance. Hélène, who stays out of these digressions, brings us back to the topic at hand and tells Hervé that before moving to a cave he should persevere with the method. Meaning he should follow the rules and stop going out at night.

'I know . . . But staying home just waiting to fall asleep, I just can't do it anymore!' he protests.

The man has clearly spoken from his heart and not his

head. Hervé hides his face behind his long fingers. He has the hands of a pianist and, for a fleeting moment, I see the silhouette of the man in the bar at Christmas – the graceful hands he used to gesticulate as he spoke. Is it really possible that Herve could have some sort of secret night life? An unconventional existence no one would ever suspect?

Jacques's deep voice interrupts my inner musings. 'Do you really think I have cut back on my sleeping pills?' he growls. 'It's hell getting out of bed with a minimum of 7mg of Zopiclone coursing through my veins.'

'Jacques, that's not what we agreed,' Hélène objects.

Our blatant defiance finally causes her to lose her legendary calm.

I wonder why none of us has reacted positively to the method. Why don't we do a better job of following the rules? Why are we so reluctant to follow any other path? Usually Michèle makes up for the rest of us, but today she's just as defeated as we are. Hélène reclaims our attention, doing her best not to raise her voice. She admits it may be necessary to be a bit more flexible with our hours and calculates new ones for each of us. Hervé's allowed to nap again. A bit late for that, I think to myself, feeling bad for him, but at least he'll be in better shape to find a new job. Michèle gets her two-hour lie-in back, and Jacques can sleep until eight o'clock. When it comes to Lena, Hélène's less convinced and asks her to continue with her current schedule until the next meeting, in a month's time.

As for me . . . It's nine o'clock and the session is over. I think Hélène, who has a hard time understanding my nightly rhythm, is relieved.

She leaves first, offering encouragements as she gets ready and urges us to stay at home at night as she steps out of the room. I help Michèle rinse the mugs. I'm glad to have an excuse to talk to her as I'm worried. It's not like her to be so sad. She laughs quietly and thanks me for asking. She says her nightmares have been terrible lately. She's too afraid to go to sleep. 'The insomnia will get the better of me in the end,' she sobs quietly. I tell her that if she gives up, the rest of us might as well throw in the towel. Above all else, I tell her to sleep, to take a pill, just for once. God won't hold it against her if she stands him up for one night.

'Maybe God won't, but my children will,' she says.

I let her leave first. Standing in front of the attic window, I study the city rooftops. There's no use denying it – I'm sinking. I'm beyond exhausted and nightfall makes me just as anxious as ever. I can't do anything anymore but work. I'm overwhelmed by fear, but this time it's unlike any other fear I've ever known. I'm afraid of falling into the abyss that has ripped the floor apart right in front of me. It's bottomless . . .

I jump as I realise I'm not alone in the room. Lena is still sitting at the table, her head resting on her forearms. I'm tempted to leave and pretend I didn't notice her but decide to ask her to have coffee with me instead. I'll make her eat a croissant and ask her why she's not in class.

If I succeed, my day won't have been a total waste.

Monday, 1.15 a.m. The phone rings. He's been waiting – she started up again after the New Year. He doesn't get out of bed. The silence has had an extra bite to it since his family left after Christmas. His wife didn't even stay for twenty-four hours – she had a mindfulness conference to go to in London. She told him, in a tone of voice he found exasperating – the sort of tone that meditation fanatics always use when they speak – that she probably wouldn't come back again. She placed her hand on his cheek, stroked his poorly shaven skin, and explained that her life now lay elsewhere. She was worried about him, she added. He seemed to be absent, and so very tired. She, on the other hand, was radiant. She'd grown more beautiful with age and her happiness only heightened her appeal. Of course she didn't want him anymore. He'd neglected her for years. Why doesn't he try to win her back, promise to change, try to make her believe that things will be different? Because he doesn't believe it himself. He'd rather be alone to watch his decline. He hopes his children didn't notice anything. He definitely felt there had been a happy atmosphere – except, that is, for Catherine, who shut herself away in the bedroom to talk on the phone every fifteen minutes, and a few conversations about economic decline, which nearly brought he and his sons to blows. No, it all went off pretty well. He didn't do such a bad job.

2 a.m. The phone again. The calls, which come increasingly late at night, have disturbed Jacques's habits. It was easier a few weeks ago, when his instructions to go to bed at midnight lined up with the call. Now he can't fall asleep until after she's called. The phone keeps ringing this time. She's determined. This doesn't bode well. She's leaving him enough time to walk through all the rooms to his office. She must know the exhaustion slows him down, and she's decided to wait. He reaches his desk at last. His hand trembles over the receiver. He picks up.

'Marie?'

There's silence on the line, but he knows she's there.

'It's late,' he continues. 'People don't make phone calls at this time of night, you know.'

'I don't sleep anymore. I've lost all track of time,' she finally explains.

Jacques barely recognises her hoarse voice, it's so full of despair.

'And you want me to suffer the same fate, I suppose?'

'My calls aren't what's keeping you awake,' she replies scathingly.

It's unlike her.

'Can I do something to help?' Jacques asks.

'Please don't. Remember what happened the last time you tried?'

'I did my duty as a doctor.'

'You can't imagine how it destroyed me. I'm nothing now. I don't exist anymore.'

'All right,' says Jacques, taking a deep breath as he tries to concentrate. 'Explain it to me. We'll talk about it if you like, OK, Marie?'

But no one is on the line. She's hung up. The Marie he used to know is gone. There's no joy or kindness there anymore. Her repeated calls suddenly scare him. Should he warn someone? The police? The psychiatric ward at a hospital? Jacques lies down on the sofa in his office. He's spent plenty of nights here. After late-night conversations with patients, he used to lie down and sleep through until morning.

As he dozes he thinks back to their first session, a year and a half ago. For six months she came to see him twice a week, hoping to resolve the severe anxiety she'd been experiencing since the birth of her daughter. The baby was only three months old when he first started seeing her. He liked Marie right away – not often the case with his patients. She was a discreet young woman and a gentle soul; shy, but disarmingly honest, which made her very approachable. He didn't need any particular strategy to get through to her – she shared everything with him without any game-playing. She was an open book. Clever and well-read, too, but free of any arrogance. Something about her inspired humility in him – an infrequent feeling for Jacques, but one that did him good. Her sincerity beckoned him to climb down from his pedestal. She didn't care about his reputation, and he discovered that was a relief. As their sessions progressed, he stepped outside the strict psychoanalytic framework and they talked about their personal lives, their musical and literary tastes, their families, and Jacques's obsession with going to bed early even though he knew he wouldn't sleep. It didn't keep them from making real progress. Marie recounted the scenarios that haunted her day and night in which her daughter always came to a terrible death. They explored her childhood, established links between generations of mothers and daughters, and as time went by, she began to feel better. But he should have been more wary of her view of herself as the all-powerful mother, the only person who knew what was best for her child. It didn't fit with the rest of the presentation of her symptoms. She refused to accept advice, believed only in alternative medicine, and avoided doctors like the plague. He failed to recognise the severity of her illness.

The office clock reads five o'clock. He resists the urge to go back to bed despite the unbearable exhaustion and Hélène's new, more flexible guidelines.

As he stands in the kitchen waiting for the kettle to whistle, he stares at the teacup in his hands and goes into a hypnotic state. The cup is from a set he and his wife brought back from Japan. He studies the delicate hand-painted floral motif and the infinite nuances of the shiny red ceramic. The cup takes advantage of his ecstatic trance and a slight but voluntary relaxing of his muscles to escape his hand and shatter into a thousand vermilion pieces on the black-and-white tile floor. Only marginally surprised, Jacques looks down at the debris. Then he calmly and slowly uses his index finger to slide the sugar bowl towards the edge of the table and, with an imperceptible push, sends it to join the cup on the floor. The beautiful teapot is about to meet the same fate when he hears a ring and jumps. But it's not the phone. It's the door.

'Catherine! Don't you have your keys?' he asks.

'It's so early, I thought . . . I mean, I didn't want to bother you,' she explains.

'Don't be silly. This is your home, too.'

'I'm just here for a few things. I'm sorry. I also wanted to tell you that I don't want any of it – none of the furniture or knick-knacks. I don't need any of it anymore.'

She refuses to stay for tea and leaves with a huge suitcase.

That may have been the last time she comes here, thinks Jacques as he stands in the hallway contemplating his reflection in the Louis XV mirror resting against the wall. The man who stares back at him is hideous.

In a fit of rage, he takes the mirror with both hands and throws it to the wooden floor. There's barely even a scratch on the patinaed frame, so he picks up a small wooden African statue from the dresser, kneels, and again goes after the object that revealed such a revolting image. He manages to break it, along with the statue. Sweating and out of breath, he stands up, satisfied with his victory. Then he heads to the kitchen to drink his cold tea. He's about to leave the room, then changes his mind and goes back to the table and sends the teapot crashing to the floor.

Tuesday, 2:20 a.m. Michèle is frustrated. She's sitting on a pew at the back of the nave, but a strange feeling has disturbed her nightly ritual. Tonight the children are out of reach. Their voices, which were so very close on her recent visits, are imperceptible now. She can't bring herself to accomplish her usual tasks. Her limbs feel numb, her body heavy. She can't even pick up a broom or duster. She tries to keep the relentless exhaustion at bay, but her head keeps falling on to her chest as sleep wins out.

3 a.m. She wakes up with a start, as if someone's just brushed past her, and sits up in a panic, certain she's not alone. A murmur reaches her from the far end of the aisle. The poor terrified woman doesn't dare leave her pew. She looks around, but neither the woman in trainers nor anyone else is around. The murmur seems to get closer, but she can't tell where it's coming from. Suddenly, she feels an invisible hand stroke her cheek. Michèle wants to scream, but a weak sigh is all she can manage. She finally stands up and runs away, forgetting to blow out the three candles. Her hands are shaking so badly she can barely lock the door and put the key back in its hiding place. She wants to keep running in the alleyway, but her legs no longer obey her brain. She considers confiding in a passer-by, asking for help, but with what exactly? Help getting home? They'd think she was mad and take her to the police station, and then her husband would know. She keeps walking, alone, dragging her fear along with her like a ball and chain.

Once Michèle is safe in her kitchen, sitting at the wooden table with a steaming cup of verbena tea clutched between her hands, she finally catches her breath and begins to calm down. But the remaining terror is enough to make her heart race. She doesn't understand. What happened? Did someone else visit the church tonight? Did she hear footsteps in her half-sleep that might explain her sudden panic? Maybe a homeless person tried to attack her? But she doesn't remember seeing anyone, just feeling the hand on her cheek. She gets up and makes her way towards her room. She slips into her nightdress and slides under the sheets. She stays sitting up, propped up on her pillows, listening to her husband's regular breathing. From behind her half-closed eyes, something intrigues her. It's dark, but the moonlight streaming through the window is enough for her to make out a brighter colour emerging from the darkness, at ground level. She sits up straight to see better. That's it, two bright pink – no, fuchsia – trainers. When Michèle looks up she can see her standing by the window and staring straight at her. The woman from church.

Her blood freezes in her veins, but her heart beats faster. She tells herself she's imagining it – it's a dream, a nightmare. She closes her eyes and counts to ten before opening them a sliver, placing her hands over them, just in case, as if she were watching a horror film. The woman has gone. But there's something else now, and the feeling it arouses is much greater than fear. They are here in her room, unmoving, at the foot of her bed. White and still. Their lips flutter as if they're trying to tell her something, but she can't hear them. Michèle wants to scream. Terrified, she tries to reach out for her sleeping husband, but her limbs are completely paralysed. Her heart is pounding so hard, her chest hurts. Sweat pearls on her brow. Then one of them moves, holding his arm out towards her. No, please, thinks Michèle. He slowly steps closer, leaving the others behind to walk around the bed. She closes her eyes. She buries her head under her pillow, stifles her sobs, and holds perfectly still. A few seconds later, everything goes black. Perhaps she passed out, or just fell asleep.

In the early morning, when she wakes up, everything looks normal again. A bold ray of sunshine streams through the curtains onto her bed. She hears her husband singing in the kitchen as the smell of toasted bread reaches her nose.

Wednesday, 4 a.m. Lena's lying in bed, holding a letter in her hands. She makes sure her brother is still asleep, then takes her phone out from under her pillow. Her father answers on the third ring. His voice is happy, though it sounds very far away and there's a lot of static on the line. Lena bites her lip. She's almost forgotten how much she misses his presence in their flat. She regrets calling and hangs up, angry. The phone vibrates several times but she doesn't answer. It's easy for him. Does he even know what she's going to college for or what her life's been like since he left? Does he know that her mother almost never goes out and does nothing but complain all day? The worst bit is that she can't even be angry with him. She loves him too much.

Lena gets up, picks her brother's stuffed toy up off the floor and watches the street outside. A baggy T-shirt falls just above the knees of her pale, skin-and-bones legs. She feels too weak to go out this morning, despite all the emotions boiling inside her. She wants to break the window, break anything, take it out on someone. Her exams are coming up soon and her chances of passing are dwindling by the day. She's doomed to fail and she's full of rage about it. Her mother has already started circling newspaper ads for demeaning jobs. There's no way out. She has to make money, or her brother won't even get a chance at higher education. And her mother won't be able to pay the bills. Lena feels trapped but doesn't know who to hold accountable anymore. She goes back to bed, completely despondent. She'll pretend to be ill, so she doesn't have to go to class. She could wander the streets, but the very idea of it exhausts her. Maybe she could convince Franck that her teachers are on strike, or sick. That way she could spend the day somewhere warm, pretending to study as she watches the other customers and eavesdrops on their conversations. Lena throws off her covers. She can't stay in this room. She takes off her T-shirt and puts on her clothes from yesterday, which are strewn across the floor. She skips her usual bathroom ritual, grabs her bag, and leaves the flat.

Thursday, 1:15 a.m. Hervé is deep in thought, though his neutral expression gives nothing away. His eyes are nearly closed, so it looks as if he's dozed off. His full glass sits on

the table surrounded by his folder, his sleep log and a notebook open to a page full of columns of words. A group at
the neighbouring table is enthusiastically discussing the play
they've just seen. When he opens his eyes she's standing in
front of him, wrapped warmly in her duffle coat, addressing
him softly. He's not all that surprised – the night always offers
a fair share of mystery.

'So it *was* you I saw the other night,' she says.

Hervé watches as she takes off her coat, gloves and hat then
smooths her hair. Her movements are unhurried and precise.

'You must know a lot of people here if you're a regular,'
she ventures.

'Not really. I keep to myself mostly,' he replies.

'You look tired.'

'Same to you.'

'That's not what I meant. You look tired, but different . . .'

If they'd had this conversation after a group meeting or in
the street in broad daylight, he would have been petrified.
Palpitations, a cold sweat, stuttering. But he's not embarrassed
here. They're on equal footing, on neutral ground. And,
luckily, she talks enough for the both of them.

'I can't put my finger on it. Your hair, your manner . . .
Less tense, maybe,' she explains.

Hervé focuses on her dimples without paying much attention to what she's saying. He's good at pretending to listen
so that he can really study the person across from him. He's
better at deciphering body language than actual words.

'You're no more talkative at night than you are during the
day,' she concludes.

'True.'

'Is this your notebook? Do you write?'

'No, insomniacs who spend their nights creating master-
pieces are the stuff of films. Take it. Maybe you'll put it to
better use.'

Hervé rips out a few scrawled-on pages and hands the notebook to Claire.

'You're right,' she agrees. 'In the real world, insomnia is much less romantic. Why do they insist on lying to people?'

'To make the whole world believe not sleeping is cool,' he suggests nonchalantly.

Claire laughs wholeheartedly and slides the notebook into her bag. Hervé blushes with satisfaction and dares to ask what she's doing here, so far from home. He regrets it immediately when her face darkens.

'I wanted to see what it was like to leave home in the middle of the night,' she explains. 'Are you heading out?'

'No, I'll stay a while longer,' Hervé replies. He can see that she looks more relaxed now.

'I'm sorry about your job. I'm sure you'll find a new one quickly,' she says encouragingly.

His job. He hasn't thought about being sacked since Claire turned up tonight. He should really get home, scour the job ads, and work on his CV rather than sitting here spending money. And staying out won't help him get to sleep either. It'll show in his interviews. Hervé starts to squirm on the bench. He feels too hot and his breathing is shallow. Claire realises her mistake and steps in to smooth things over. She orders two glasses of wine, without asking him first. The alcohol helps calm Hervé down as Claire confides in him. She talks about the permanent exhaustion that dictates her life, how she's let herself go. She doesn't even dare go to the hairdresser anymore because she can't bear to look at herself in the mirror, much less hold a conversation. But her hair is a disaster. Before, with Paul, she would make an effort to style it, especially when they went out together. He used to find her pretty sometimes, but now . . .

'No, you haven't let yourself go,' interrupts Hervé. 'You're on a bridge between two worlds, and the abyss between them is dizzying. Your hair is lovely. Let it do as it pleases.'

Claire is silent as she awkwardly runs her hand over her hair, as if to confirm Hervé's assertions.

It's after three o'clock when they part company. For the entire walk home, Hervé keeps wondering what he was on about with his silly bridge.

Friday, 3 a.m. The shouting has started up again in the next room. A baby has been screaming for an hour, and the comings and goings in the stairwell create a constant din. Peals of laughter from a group that has been loitering right under my window for the past hour has my nerves on edge. As soon as things quieten down, I start listening for them to pick up again. When they do, I sit bolt upright in bed. I could go and meet up with Hervé, but by the time I got there he'd probably be gone. I must admit he was anything but boring last night. In the end, the accountant was rather talkative. More laughter. Why haven't I looked for a quieter place to stay? After all, I have no intention of going home.

The decision wasn't so hard to make in the end. It's the sort of thing you build up in your mind, but then, when it comes to it, you just do it and it's over. When I went home, just before dawn, after my theatrical Christmas Day disappearance, the fight I had expected never came. Paul didn't say anything. He'd given up on talking. His aggrieved expression said it all. I could hear him shouting on the inside, and it was somehow worse. *You've gone mad! You can't just disappear like that! Do you realise how worried I was, how uncomfortable it was for me with my parents? And especially for Thomas. How could you? He's just a kid!* I could hear his silent reproaches clear as day. This time I'd gone too far. Our lives were too out of sync. I didn't say anything, didn't bother to defend myself. I felt numb, with a knot in the pit of my stomach. When Paul went back upstairs I grabbed a pile of dirty plates off the table and dropped them on the floor. A pitiful attempt at revolt – I could at least have thrown them across the room. Then I sat down amid the debris and cried until the sun came up. It wasn't the pathetic nature of the situation, but the absolute emptiness of it that overwhelmed me, the unbearable absence of a shoulder to lean on for even an instant.

One night, after a few days of radio silence – Paul was avoiding me even more than usual, as if I'd become a potential danger, a ticking time bomb – I waited for Thomas to go to sleep, then packed my bag, certain of a decision I'd finally made after months of hesitation. I felt nothing. I would have liked to feel something – sadness at least, as a tribute to all my past emotions – but I didn't shed a tear. Paul made no effort to get me to stay. He just said wearily that my insomnia made me inaccessible, that it was pointless to try to love someone as neurotic as me, that he'd tried to help me but couldn't take it anymore. I let him speak despite my outrage at his lack of sincerity. When I tried to look him in the eyes he looked away. The conversation was over. Paul went to bed, without a word, as if we'd see each other again at breakfast. I stood motionless at the kitchen window for a while.

I took the last train into the city and went back to the same hotel. The receptionist winked at me when he saw me turn up with my suitcase. I ignored him and asked for the same room. I'm not sleeping any better, of course. Although I used to complain about the silence in the house, here the noise never stops. Anxiety about my vulnerability as a single, homeless woman keeps me up all night. I can't spend the rest of my life in a hotel. I need to find a flat, a studio – something. I've got to find more clients now, too, since I can't rely on

Paul's earnings anymore. I thought my decision to leave would make me stronger and boost my energy. But now, alone in my room, I'm afraid things may not turn out any better. My only consolation is that I'm free of worried, guilt-inducing looks. And that I don't have to listen to anyone snore next to me anymore. Other than that, I'm terribly lonely.

I stopped caring about my sleep schedule a while ago and started sleeping during the day. But I'm still going to the meetings, which have become my only tie to the rest of the world. I even look forward to them. Hervé's face pops into my head again. The one from last night, which is strangely different from his stricken daytime expression. Deeper, almost brooding.

4.30 a.m. More loud voices, then a woman roars with laughter. My heart is trapped in a vice. I need to sleep. I jump out of bed to rifle through my toiletries bag for the bottle of Benadryl. I always have one on hand just in case – it reassures me, and helps a little when things get really bad. But the little pink bottle is nowhere to be found. I dump all the bag's contents on to the bathroom floor and panic takes hold of me as I realise I'm not going to find it. I collapse onto the linoleum floor and furiously start throwing everything in my path. At least no one will notice here. I sit down on the bed. I'm in the city, and you can always find whatever you need in the city, even in the middle of the night. A chemist. There has got to be a 24-hour chemist somewhere. I grab my mobile and miraculously manage to find a chemist that's open, and, even better, it's only twenty minutes away on foot, though I would have walked for an hour.

In front of me in the queue there are exhausted parents with an A&E prescription in hand, a drug addict, whom the security guard quickly removes from the premises, and a young man holding a bloody compress to his face. At last it's my turn. The pharmacist – a balding Asian man with dead eyes and skin with a strange green pallor – goes above and beyond the call of duty, recommending several plant-based and essential oil treatments. He speaks quietly. It takes all the restraint I can muster to hold back from telling him where he can shove his herbal teas. I repeat that I'll just take the Benadryl.

He turns around with a sigh to get the medicine. I put my bank card in the reader and enter my PIN without a second thought. *Incorrect PIN.* I must have made a mistake. I start again, my nerves fraying. Second attempt: *Incorrect PIN.* I feel my heart pounding in my chest as beads of sweat begin to gather on my brow. This can't be happening, I never forget my PIN number – I know it like my own name. The pharmacist warns me that if I get it wrong again, my card will be frozen. I need the meds; I have to sleep. I'm sure I'll remember correctly this time – there's no reason why I shouldn't, but the numbers start spinning and my certainty fades away. I can't leave empty-handed. I'm shaking and my heart is beating too fast. Here goes nothing. Third try: *Incorrect PIN.* 'Shit!' I shout out loud without realising it. The security guard sizes me up, ready to intervene. I beg the man behind the counter, who seems a bit jumpy now. 'Please, I'll come back and pay you tomorrow. I'll leave you my ID card.' He shakes his head. I go back out into the street, on the verge of a nervous breakdown, and curse the entire world.

When I get back to my room, I stand at the window. The sky is slowly getting brighter despite a light drizzle. My breathing slows down. The waiter at the café across the street brings the tables out on to the pavement and opens the awning. The neon sign attracts the first customers of the day. I watch as the street comes to life. In the room next door, I hear an alarm go off.

7

Monday 8.10 a.m. The room is silent. Hervé is sitting up straight on his chair, his gaze directed towards the window, his glasses slightly askew. When he sees me walk in he carefully avoids looking in my direction, so I mischievously stare at him, trying to force his hand.

Hélène is sitting next to him studying her files.

'Are those the assessments of our nights?' I ask.

'Strange, isn't it?' she replies. 'The inability to sleep, I mean?'

To my surprise her voice is much warmer than usual, almost friendly. The change is slight, but noticeable enough for me to see her as more than just a teacher who subjects her students to brutal and poorly suited methods. Today she seems more like a woman who loves her job and sincerely wants to help.

'It's a mystery, all right,' I concede. 'But why have we all failed?'

'You're a complex group. It's rather rare,' she explains.

'You must be used to difficult cases, though, right?'

'Each insomniac is unique and deserves a great deal of time and interest. Unfortunately, we don't have enough funding for that so we do what we can.'

'Does sleep restriction really work?' I ask doubtfully.

'Definitely – it's tried and tested. Why else would I make you all struggle through it for weeks? Let's get started. The others can join in when they get here. Wake up, Jacques!'

Jacques, whom I hadn't even noticed up till now, stands

up laboriously. He seems to age significantly between sessions. He moves slowly towards the table, his eyes scanning the space for the thermos of coffee. But Michèle isn't here yet, which worries me. It's not like her to be late. Hélène studies our sleep logs and has a hard time hiding her disappointment. I wish I had been more diligent.

Michèle finally turns up and everyone can see there's a difference in her face – she's pale, with huge dark circles under her blue eyes. Her expression is even more troubling: totally blank, unable to focus on anything. Clearly concerned, Hélène asks her what's happened. Michèle momentarily sheds her listlessness to say hello in a jolly voice that doesn't fool anyone, then pulls the thermos out of her bag as if nothing has changed.

'Thank you,' says Jacques. 'You're saving my life with this coffee.'

'Bad night, Jacques?' Michèle teases.

The session begins. I keep my eye on Michèle, trying to guess what she's hiding behind her mask. Hélène congratulates her enthusiastically for not going to church for the past several nights. The sleep log has spoken.

'Like I said, Michèle, they're always in your heart, wherever you are. And at night, the best place to be is your bedroom,' Hélène affirms triumphantly.

Michèle goes even paler. The air is rife with tension. She's our rock. The optimistic insomniac who manages to get through the day no matter what. If she falls, our hope falls with her.

Lena arrives, out of breath, her cheeks flushed from the cold. 'Why so quiet? Have you seen a ghost or something?' she asks with her usual tact.

Michèle puts her head in her hand. Here we go – she's about to lose it. I place my hand on her arm and encourage her to tell us what's wrong. She looks up at us, her eyes full of terror.

'You're not far off, Lena,' she finally says.

Jacques snaps to attention.

'I was only joking,' says Lena, suddenly less sure of herself.

'I see them,' reveals Michèle, full of despair. 'I see our children, like I see all of you. They appear before me every night, in the flesh. I can't take it anymore! Maybe I've finally gone mad. You were right, Jacques.'

'It takes time to make a diagnosis,' the psychiatrist replies dryly.

'That's fantastic,' Lena says earnestly.

'It's terrifying,' counters Michèle.

'Where is it that you think you see these ghosts?' asks Hélène, who doesn't seem particularly concerned.

'Everywhere! At church, in my room – their dark eyes stare at me every night. But it's as if they're no longer my children. I can't talk to them anymore.'

Her voice shakes. Have the sleepless nights finally got the better of the poor woman? Hélène takes over the conversation, her voice calm, even and professional. 'Listen to me, Michèle. You're not crazy. They aren't ghosts. They're hypnagogic hallucinations.'

'What the hell are they?' asks Lena.

'They're hallucinations that occur as you're falling asleep. Just before you lose consciousness, when you can still access all five senses. Most of the time the visions seem real as they are terrifying. They can be accompanied by voices, sounds and physical sensations. Sometimes the person who experiences them can't move.'

Michèle takes no comfort in this rational explanation. 'But I'm not dreaming when I'm at church, or when I go to bed!' she protests.

'That's what you think, Michèle. But don't forget, you're not sleeping very much, and your body has to make up for it somehow, maybe without you realising it. You could easily pass out from exhaustion whenever you sit down, even if only for a few seconds. I understand your distress, but it's nothing to worry about. I think you should stop going to church at night altogether. Your visits are creating disturbing images for your unconscious mind.'

Jacques defends Hélène's position, trying to soothe the poor, suffering woman. I'm surprised by his act of kindness, which seems totally out of character. But nothing seems to convince Michèle. She's devastated. I imagine that behind the terrible fear, there must be something else as well. The loss of her imaginary children.

The rest of the session continues in an atmosphere of mourning. We all speak softly and are particularly attentive to Michèle, who, with our support, slowly regains her composure. We all have times when we let down the tall, strong walls we've built around ourselves – rare occasions when we feel we won't be judged and let it all out. Sometimes – as in those drunken discussions where you forget to hold back – we regret it afterwards. But it's too late, it's been said. And it helps us feel better for a moment.

For the first time, Jacques talks about his private life. He tells us about his wife, who left him just after the New Year. She doesn't answer his calls anymore and hasn't told him a thing about her new life. He doesn't even know if she's met someone. But he imagines she has – Catherine is beautiful and doesn't like to be alone. He's tried in vain to get the details from his children. Touched by his sudden humility, I keep my sarcastic comments to myself.

Lena takes a picture of a new-born out of her pocket and Michèle fawns over the little bundle of joy. 'My dad's baby,' Lena announces dryly. This is the first thing that comes to mind every morning when she wakes up. It drives her mad to know that now it's this little girl that her father kisses before going to work. Despite her best efforts, she hates the child and refuses to visit. Hervé notices a resemblance in the eyes and the shape of her mouth. Lena grabs the photo back and looks closer. Clever Hervé, I think to myself.

Hélène, who's realised there's no point analysing our sleep logs today, works discreetly on her files until the clock tells us the meeting is over.

Tuesday, 12.30 am. Michèle rests her head in her hands. Hélène is wrong – they're not hallucinations. Her children are here in the flesh. She never wanted this, though. She never wanted them to be anything more than childlike voices joyfully breaking the silence of the empty church. Voices in her head. She lies down on a pew in the small chapel at the far end of the church. Dozens of candles are still burning. Her fear grows with each new apparition. The woman in trainers has taken up her usual place across from the choir, along with a few other people this time, and Michèle waves shyly to them, her hand shaking. She always sees the woman first, before her own children, and has decided she must be some sort of guardian of the dead. The twins, glued to one another like Siamese twins from a horror film, terrify her – their pale faces a far cry from the cheerful expressions Michèle has always imagined when speaking to them. Her imaginary children are more human than these threatening strangers from another dimension, whom she now sees nightly. They haven't spoken a word to her since the night when they appeared for the first time at the foot of her bed. Michèle can feel herself sinking into depression again. She doesn't dare mention it to the priest – much less her husband, who hasn't even seemed to notice the changes in his wife's behaviour. What if these visions are a clue that she's possessed? She saw the devil once, why not ghosts? Maybe these children are dead people who haunt her nights. *Dear God, please* *help me. Save me from the abyss I'm about to fall into.* She opens her eyes a sliver. She can make out the three demons, still in the same place, staring at her, as if waiting for her to do something.

Michèle sits up and tries to reason with herself. A few minutes later she bravely opens her eyes fully and looks straight at them. Why would they want to hurt her? They're only children. Maybe she just needs to win them over, by showing them a little love and affection. That's all children ever want. God is sending her a message. *They've come to bring you back from the darkest night. Trust them.* She stands up tall, giving herself a little more confidence. She walks towards them slowly, no longer afraid of their insistent gaze, doing her best to hide any residual fear. She manages to hold out her hand and stroke their cheeks. She can feel their warm breath on her skin. *My children, my beloved children . . .*

Tuesday, 12:10 a.m. The din at the hotel reaches a peak. A muffled sound coming from the room next door makes me jump. The atmosphere has become worrying. The relatively tame daytime setting quickly turns into a nightmare when the sun goes down. I venture out into the corridor. It's the police trying to break down the door. 'Don't stay there, ma'am. The man might be armed. Take what you need and go out until we've handled the situation.' There's no need to ask me twice – the shouting from inside the room leads me to fear the worst – and I quickly grab my bag, swearing I'll move hotels tomorrow.

A small crowd has formed outside. It's cold and I have no desire to wait here for the situation to be 'handled', nor to come back to a crime scene.

I think of how upset Michèle was at our last meeting. This vision business is disturbing. Has she really lost it? I hesitate for a few minutes, then decide to go to her. I know where to find her sanctuary.

This neighbourhood is always so busy during the day, but now the street is deserted. The main door is locked so I walk around the building to find another entrance, which leads to a pitch-black hallway. I take a few steps with my arms held out in front of me and manage to find my way into the church. Three candles are burning near the entrance, set apart from the others. Michèle is here. Without thinking, I light a fourth. The chairs are in perfectly straight rows and the church is in total silence. I can see why Michèle comes here. Whatever god you believe in or convictions you hold, peace is universal. The world is kept at bay outside by the heavy doors. Sleep must be easier to come by in the candlelit alcoves. My senses, usually on high alert at this time of night, are soothed by the stained glass windows colouring the stone floor and the smell of incense. I sit down and close my eyes to take in the aura of this holy place more deeply and almost forget the reason for my visit.

A voice coming from the back of the church reminds me of my mission. The faint echo guides me to the darkest part of the church: a small chapel lit by a thousand candles. Michèle has her back to me. She's talking, mumbling something. I can barely hear her, but her gestures trouble me. I can almost make out a human shape outlined by her movements. She gets down on her knees, as if to be eye level with a child, then wraps her arms around invisible narrow shoulders and brushes her lips against invisible cheeks. 'My darlings, my beloved children, how I've missed you. I love you so very much.' I can feel tears welling in my eyes and clench my jaw to keep them from flowing freely. The children are real for a moment, and I feel an emptiness within, a terrible void. As I contemplate the mystical scene, music breaks the silence that fills the church. The sound is so pure it's unreal. I don't know if Michèle is pulling me into her madness, or if the lack of sleep has altered our consciousness, but I don't really care. The tall, thin silhouette communing with those who are missing from her life, whose absence has traumatised her, the soul-wrenching violin melody – this scene is sacred. I watch Michèle, thinking of the children she'll never have and of those I never wanted. I think of Thomas, whom I failed as a stepmother.

She still has her back to me, though she's no longer moving. Her hands are joined in prayer and I imagine her eyes are closed. The intensity of her devotion is palpable. I turn around as quietly as possible. When I reach the choir I cross paths with a man in a tuxedo sitting on a chair with his music stand in front of him. In one hand he holds his violin, in the other a can of beer. He jumps up as if he's just seen a ghost. That said, I can't blame him. The lack of sleep has really affected my appearance. My complexion is now almost as pale as Lena's, and my cheeks are hollow. The purple circles under my eyes really do make me look like a zombie.

I offer him the friendliest smile I can manage. 'What was that?' I ask.

'Concerto for Violin in E minor, Mendelssohn, Opus 64,' mumbles the man under his breath.

I imagine how he'll react when he runs into an old woman who talks to herself.

1.30 a.m. It takes me a few minutes to adapt to the real world. I lean back against the church façade and light a cigarette. I watch the few passers-by, studying their gait, eavesdropping on bits of conversation. I look up at the windows with lights on and realise that Michèle really is losing her mind. I promise to do my best to bring her back to the world of the living. Even if it means discussing it with Jacques, to get a professional opinion.

I can't bear the idea of going back to my seedy hotel. I almost regret leaving Paul; I don't have a home, or a comfortable bed, or anyone to welcome me. I call Françoise but get her voicemail. I forgot, she's abroad on tour; Paul doesn't ever contact me. Ten years together and he doesn't even worry about me. Thomas is the one I really miss, though. I'd like to talk to him, explain that I had no choice and that if he had been my son, I would have brought him with me. We would have worked it out, with joint custody, like everyone else. I make my way towards Hervé's bar, hoping to find him there.

Tuesday, 1 a.m. Hervé is staring at the café door. He rarely follows his intuition. In fact, he never really feels it. But this time he knows she'll be here. He's come every night since they ran into each other. He doesn't even bother trying to sleep. He listens to the radio until midnight, then puts on his pyjamas and gets into bed out of principle, because there are certain rituals that can't be changed. Then, at one o'clock, he gets up, gets dressed, and comes here to wait for her.

He has a plan: he's made a strange discovery and wants to share it with Claire. He has to tell someone. And who else could he confide in from the group? But maybe their first meeting has put her off going out at night? He should have stayed at home to prepare for his job interview – it's his only chance. He watches the minutes tick past on his mobile. He opens his inbox out of habit, but it's always empty now. After losing his job, Hervé has decided to lead a regimented life – he can't neglect everything as if he were on holiday. He gets up at eight o'clock, regardless of the number of hours he's slept. He showers and eats breakfast, then goes out for groceries. When he gets home, he prepares an elegant meal, which he often doesn't eat. His anxiety has destroyed his stomach. He may even have an ulcer – he should probably go to see a doctor, but he's not sure he'd hold up if the diagnosis was bad news. He spends the rest of the day looking for a job, giving it his all. Since he was fired for professional misconduct he doesn't get unemployment benefit. The agency gave him a small severance package, out of guilt, but it won't last long. He has to find something quickly.

The woman at the bar keeps glancing longingly in Hervé's direction, but he's careful to avoid meeting her eyes. She'd think it was a sign. Though the experience was mostly positive, he doesn't want a repeat.

2 a.m. The number of customers in the café dwindles as the night draws in. He's beginning to feel perfectly ridiculous and is about to put on his trench coat when Claire finally arrives. A few curly strands of hair have escaped from her woollen hat. Her features are drawn, but the cool spring air has left her nose and cheeks red, bringing colour to her face. She heads towards his table and calmly says hello. Hervé starts to stutter, then gets a handle on things and invites her to sit down. He has to speak first, or he won't dare interrupt her. She sits down and puts her head in her hands without saying a word. Hervé wants to laugh because her hat has left her hair looking rather silly.

'Want something to distract you?' he asks.

Without waiting for her reply he tells her the whole story, everything since the first night when he randomly made the discovery on his way home. Claire seems sceptical. It's easy to mistake a cat for a dog in the dark, even when you're not exhausted, so he probably shouldn't put too much faith in his senses.

Hervé is disappointed. He thought she would be curious, but she doesn't seem the least bit interested. He decides to persevere, but he gets all mixed up when he tells the story.

He's no good at long, coherent conversations – he'll just have to show her. He suggests they go. Right away. But she turns him down. Rushing through the cold streets in the dark isn't her cup of tea. However, his unexpected tenacity eventually pays off.

He stands up nervously and leads Claire outside. He strides along the dimly lit street, his gait becoming more confident with each lengthening step. His open trench coat flaps in the wind and he holds his head high, like a man reborn. Even his curly hair has a new vitality to it. Claire barely recognises the withered man from the group meetings – she feels as if she's watching the metamorphosis of a tortured man into a nocturnal bird that's about to take flight.

He asks Claire to follow him. Fifteen minutes later, in an affluent neighbourhood, he holds out his arm then gestures for her to join him in the porch of a stone apartment building.

'This is it. Don't move,' he says. Even his voice has changed; it's deeper and more confident.

The narrow street is deserted. The neighbouring buildings are all dark – except for the one just across the road from their hiding place. When she looks closely, Claire realises there are tiny gaps between the heavy blackout curtains covering the windows that let slivers of light shine through. Most people wouldn't notice, but it's clear that no one is asleep inside. Over the course of an hour, three people go into the building. Then she finally comes out. Claire can't believe her eyes. Hervé is quietly delighted by her surprise.

'OK, I admit it's unexpected, but she's allowed to leave her home whenever she likes,' Claire finally ventures.

'I don't think this is where she lives. Follow me.'

They begin tailing her. Hervé is quite comfortable doing it. He knows how to keep the right distance, anticipate her movements, and step into a doorway whenever he feels their target is likely to turn around. They leave this part of the city and make their way to an adjacent neighbourhood that is less affluent, where they stop for the second time. Once again they find a building that seems at first glance to be closed up for the night, but when they look closely, they can see the lights are on behind all the shutters and curtains. The woman disappears into the building, followed by an old man with a hunchback and a cane, and then a young woman who, with her slim silhouette, duffle coat, backpack and pompom beanie, looks like a student.

'She looks like you,' whispers Hervé.

'I've never worn a hat like that,' Claire replies indignantly. 'And I know I'm not very tall, but, come on, she's tiny.'

The woman emerges from the building half an hour later and gets into a taxi waiting for her in the street, then disappears into the city. The trail's gone cold. Hervé seems disappointed it's over. Afraid Claire might decide to head home, and bolstered by their nocturnal adventure, he invites her to his place for a cup of coffee – his flat's not far, and it would warm them up. He doesn't really believe she'll accept. But to his great surprise, Claire immediately agrees. Hervé has never felt so honoured, but when he sees the peeling paint in the stairwell, his audacity dwindles, and as they get closer to his floor he begins to seriously regret his offer. Claire hasn't said a word though and doesn't seem at all surprised by the state of the building.

'Here we are,' says Hervé shakily. 'I won't give you a tour since it's all in one room. Don't mind the décor.'

His small studio flat, decorated in a typical old lady's style, which is perfect for his lonely existence, seems terribly shabby now that Claire is in it. He feels like Cinderella after midnight. But she doesn't seem to notice the tacky decorations. She makes her way to the sofa and lies down. Hervé starts to relax and heads to the tiny kitchen, where he prepares two mugs of steaming coffee. He places them on the table, then goes to sit down at the foot of his bed, on the other side of the room. He does it all slowly, his back slumped in exhaustion.

'How long have you been following her?' asks Claire.

'A few weeks. I'm not exactly sure. I came across her the first time by accident.'

'What do you think she's doing? What's going on in those buildings?'

'No idea, but let's not ask her right away. I think, in any case, it may be against the law to follow someone like that.'

'It's not illegal to run into them,' she counters.

Hervé runs his hand over his poorly shaven cheeks.

'This is a good look for you,' says Claire.

'What? Neglect?' asks Hervé, doubtfully.

Claire closes her eyes. The silence isn't the least bit awkward. Hervé retrieves a woollen blanket from a closet and gently places it over this mysterious woman, who's already fast asleep. He goes to bed but is unable to fall asleep himself. Her presence troubles him. He's not sure if it's disturbing or a nice change. Both, he decides, after thinking on it for a few minutes. Without knowing why, he picks up his phone and taps out a message: *Hey, son, how are you doing?*

Two hours later, he gets up without a sound, takes a shower, and writes a note, which he leaves on the table.

Meeting at unemployment office. Fresh coffee in the kitchen. Shall we do this again soon? You know where to find me . . .

In the stairwell, his mobile vibrates. *Not bad, and you?* It's a good start, he thinks. He considers inviting his son to lunch some time soon, maybe with Claire. It would be more fun that way, he decides, as he continues down the stairs, feeling much lighter than usual.

Monday, 2 a.m. Jacques is champing at the bit. She never calls at midnight on the dot anymore, but no matter. As he

waits he methodically rips out the seams of the sofa uphol-
stery with a pair of nail scissors. His wife had been so proud
of the designer fabric when she'd found it on sale in a ware-
house. A bright yellow velvet. 'Cheery and warm, perfect for
your patients!' she'd exclaimed.

There won't be any more patients and there won't be
any more sofa soon. The cushions, piled up on the floor,
have already been stripped of their covers. The ringing
makes him jump. He drops his scissors and hastily reaches
for the telephone.

'Marie?' he asks.

'You may be able to help me after all,' she replies.

'I'm glad to hear you say that. That's a good place to start.'

'You stole her away from me, you know? And I'll never
see her again.'

'Why do you say that? You'll get her back as long as you
do what it takes to get better. And I'll help you.'

'I got a letter, after waiting for what seemed like for ever.
The judge made the decision last month. I've been refused
any form of custody and there's no possibility of an appeal.'

'What happened? Did you come off your meds? Listen to
me. Are you there?'

Sobs of unbearable pain reach his ear.

'How did I end up here?' she asks from behind her tears.

'We'll work together. You're not alone. Is there someone
you can call? You mentioned your mother several times. Ask
her to come and stay with you tonight.'

'If my mother were still alive, she'd already be by my side.'

'My sincerest condolences. When did she die?'

'When I was six.'

Jacques panics and his heart begins to race. Things are
more serious than he thought. Marie always used to talk
about her mother in the present tense. He shivers.

'How did she die?'

'A heart attack. The EMTs were unable to revive her. I was there. It was in the lounge on Christmas Eve.'

He hears her sobbing again. What an idiot! Why didn't he see it before? Any novice psychiatrist would have managed to get her to talk. Jacques takes slow, deep breaths, and uses his calmest, most reassuring voice to try to keep her with him, to console the inconsolable, and buy time to think of a solution. But he's too slow. The line's gone quiet. She's hung up yet again.

He remains seated in his armchair, slightly dizzy from his sleeping pills. Fragments of his last session with Marie begin to surface in his memory. She'd been nervous and flighty, which was rather unlike her. She was usually quite cooperative, but this time she rebuffed his attempts to connect. After three quarters of an hour, he managed to get it out of her that she was worried about her daughter's health. Her fever hadn't gone down in forty-eight hours and her coughing fits left her gasping for breath. The essential oil treatments she'd been giving the little girl didn't seem to be working. Jacques grew uncomfortable as his emotions warned him something wasn't right. The baby seemed to be suffering and the mother was losing it. He suggested she hurry home and take her daughter straight to the doctor. When she realised how worried she'd made him, Marie magically calmed down and began minimising the situation. She'd give her a few extra drops of her plant-based remedy and everything would be fine. Still concerned, Jacques had asked Marie to call him later that night, at 8 p.m., he'd finished with his last patient, to let him know everything was OK. He was relieved when she accepted.

Jacques knows he should get up and do something to help the poor woman. But remaining lucid on the phone has sapped all his energy. He feels numb and his head is spinning. The lamp seems to be dancing and it looks to him like the feet of his desk are all twisted. The sleeping pills have won. In just a few minutes he falls asleep sitting in his chair, his chin resting on his chest.

4.30 a.m. A faraway ringing, as if from another world, surprises him in his dreams. As it grows closer, the strident sound brings him back to reality. He opens his eyes, but it takes him another few seconds to emerge from his deep sleep. It's the doorbell. It's constant now, as if someone's holding the button down. Jacques gets up and drags himself to the hallway. What on earth did he take last night? He thinks he may really be hallucinating due to a sleeping pill overdose, but when he opens the door he finds two police officers in uniform along with a third in plain clothes, all standing tall as if to attention. They coldly ask him to come with them to the station immediately. If he refuses, they'll have to cuff him. In shock, with his mind still slowed by the meds, Jacques grabs his coat and a pair of trainers he finds lying about, then obediently follows the police.

Monday, 6.15 a.m. Sitting at the counter, Lena pretends to study under Franck's watchful eye. He glances approvingly at her as he wipes down the metal surface with white vinegar.

'You're bordering on OCD, Franck. You're going to scare customers away with the stench,' she warns.

'No one ever comes in this early anyway. And look how shiny it is.'

Lena rests her head on her arms and watches the first passers-by in the street. She suddenly jerks to attention and motions to Franck to come closer, then points to a man who's about to come in.

'Another bum? Don't worry, I'll take care of it,' he reassures her.

'No, it's the psychiatrist from my insomnia group!'

Franck stares at Lena, then at the man again, and bursts into fits of laughter. Lena begs him to stop, but Franck is on a roll. He has a go at making several bad jokes about psychiatrists and insomniacs.

Lena jumps up and walks over to Jacques to ask him to join her.

'I saw this café open from several blocks away. It's the only one. I thought I might find you here,' he explains.

'You know you're in your pyjamas, right?' she asks.

'There was an emergency last night . . .' replies the psychiatrist.

Lena turns back towards Franck, who's still having a hard time being serious, and orders two espressos. She gives him a dirty look. Jacques seems totally lost.

'Are you planning on going home to change before the meeting?' she asks as she glances at the clock. The bin men will be in soon, and poor Jacques will be the butt of all their jokes. Lena calls home to tell her little brother he'll have to make do on his own this morning, then offers to take Jacques home.

'No, there's no need . . .' he objects.

'You're still in your pyjamas and you can't string more than three words together. I'll call a taxi. You can take a nice warm shower and then we'll go to the meeting together.'

'Oh right, the meeting.'

Jacques doesn't resist for long. The tall, sturdy man and frail girl leave the café and climb into a cab. Uttering a string of 'wows' and 'ohs', the young woman can't contain her amazement when they enter the lobby of the Haussmann-style apartment building. She's never been inside such a high-end place. The chandelier, which could be hanging in a five-star hotel, the thick red carpet, and the marble floor in the lift all remind her of the romantic comedies she likes to watch on TV, in which the protagonists are always wealthy.

Jacques tries to open his door, but his shaking hands make it impossible. Lena takes his keys and succeeds on the first attempt. The scene that awaits them inside takes her breath away. Jacques turns on the lights and makes his way towards the lounge.

'Watch your step, Lena. I don't want you to get hurt.'

The floor is cluttered with piles of varying sizes. Pieces of wood, furniture feet, battered drawers, broken decorative objects, shards of glass, strips of fabric. They're all lined up along the walls. Not a single piece of furniture or decoration has gone unscathed.

'What the hell is this?'

'I was tired of all these things . . . My wife was right, they only distract us from what really matters. Wait for me in the lounge. I'm going to change. Make yourself a cup of coffee!'

'What a psycho,' Lena mumbles.

Jacques continues talking, his voice growing louder as the distance between them increases, to make sure Lena can still hear him, but she's too shocked to listen. What's happened here is beyond her. How could anyone voluntarily destroy their own things? Beautiful, expensive things. Still confused, she makes her way to a smaller room, which must have been a charming office before Jacques ransacked it. She hangs up the phone, which is hanging from its cord, turns off the lamp, whose glass shade lies shattered on the torn oriental rug, and lies down on the tattered sofa. So, this is what it's like, she thinks. She imagines sharing everything that's troubled her since her father left with a stranger who's paid to listen. The idea seems appealing. Two minutes later, she falls asleep.

8

Monday, 8:20 a.m. Hervé and Michèle are already here. I glance at the armchair, but Jacques isn't there. At this rate we'll soon be starting five minutes before the end of the session. Hélène welcomes me with a polite smile. I can see that our lateness must be irritating and I understand what she must think of us: we're a group of childish adults unable to take responsibility for our own wellbeing. I'm about to apologise when Jacques and Lena appear in the corridor. It's the first time they've ever arrived together. I can't help but notice the worried way the teenager keeps looking at the psychiatrist once we're all seated.

Hélène studies Jacques. 'You're very pale this morning,' she says. 'Didn't you sleep at all? Do you have your log?'

Jacques seems totally disoriented, his usual confidence and composure gone. It takes him a moment to reply. 'I was accused of murder last night,' he finally says. 'So the log wasn't exactly a priority.'

What on earth? This group has some serious problems. Michèle with her ghosts, and now Jacques with a murder. No one reacts, except for Lena, who lets out a forced laugh.

'Maybe it was a nightmare?' ventures Hélène without much conviction.

But Jacques isn't listening. He stares straight ahead blankly as he speaks. 'She called me and we talked. I should have gone to her. It was clearly a plea for help. Last night was different. She had just found out she would never get her daughter back. But I sat there unable to move. I had passed out because of the number of sleeping pills I'd taken. Not long before dawn the police showed up. They'd found an angry letter addressed to me in her flat – apparently that was enough to make me a potential suspect. They took me to a tiny windowless room and fired questions at me then told me that she had jumped out of the window and that they thought I had urged her to do it. She still had a teddy bear in her arms when they found her. Thankfully they soon realised I wasn't responsible.'

'Who was the woman?' Michèle asks quietly.

'A former patient.'

'Is this the first time one of your patients has committed suicide?'

'No, but it's never kept me up at night before.'

'And what about her daughter? What happened to her?' Michèle asks anxiously.

'She nearly died because her mother was afraid to take her to the doctor, and because I failed to see how troubled the mother was. She lives with her father now.'

'It can hardly be your fault,' argues Michèle.

'The last time I saw her, Marie finally confided that she was worried about her daughter's health. We agreed she'd call me that night to let me know how things were going. At nine o'clock I still hadn't heard from her, so I explained the barebones of the case to my wife and asked her opinion. She suggested I call Marie. When I did, I got Marie's husband on the line in a panic. The baby wasn't breathing properly and had gone limp, but Marie kept telling him everything would be OK and lost it when he suggested they needed to get her to a doctor. I adopted the firmest tone I could and threatened to send the police over if he didn't immediately overrule his wife's objections and take the baby to A&E. I hung up and called social services, then went to bed and slept all night.'

'That's it?' asks Lena incredulously. 'I would have gone to see her at least!'

'When I called the social worker the next day, she thanked me for intervening. The child had been saved just in time from severe bronchiolitis. Just a few hours later and she would have died. She informed me they had temporarily removed the girl from her mother's care until they could learn more about her mental health status. That night Marie was hysterical when she called and shouted all sorts of profanities at me – the man who had taken away her baby, her flesh and blood, her reason to live. 'How can you sleep at night after doing such a thing?' she said accusingly before hanging up. And that accusation worked like a curse. That was a year ago and she's called me at midnight every night since. Until the last few weeks, when her calls came later and became more compulsive. I finally answered the phone, realising something must have happened. It was the letter from the judge. Since she'd been charged with kidnapping after a failed attempt to take her daughter back one night, and the psychiatric evaluations were less than promising, the judge had made his decision. She was no longer permitted to see her daughter except for a few hours a month, with the father and a social worker present. It was obviously unbearable for Marie, who derived her sense of self from her status as a mother. So last night she jumped.'

'Bloody hell,' mumbles Lena.

'My sentiments precisely,' replies Jacques. 'By the way, thanks for the coffee this morning.'

'My God,' whispers Michèle, her eyes brimming with tears. 'That poor woman, the poor child . . .' She wants to get up and hug Jacques, but she knows he'd refuse her affection.

'So, to sum things up, after nine sessions, we have a psychiatrist implicated in his patient's suicide, a lady who sees ghosts – sorry Michèle, I know I'm going over the top here – a jobless accountant, a runaway (that's me) and a teenage girl who wanders the streets at dawn,' I say dryly.

'Time's up,' Hélène concludes.

It's 9.10 a.m., but no one moves.

'Don't you have class?' I ask Lena.

'I do. I'm going,' she replies, her lie too thinly veiled.

'You haven't given up, have you? Your exams are coming up, aren't they?'

'In a month. I'm studying hard.'

I don't believe a word Lena says, and the look on Michèle's face says she doesn't either.

'We should do something. We can't let her give up! Have you seen how skinny she's become?' Michèle urges quietly.

'We'll find a solution,' I whisper back, though I'm not totally convinced.

We watch as Lena leaves. I can't help but smile. Her frail frame, in a black springtime outfit revealing the nearly transparent skin of her bony shoulders and knees, looks about ready to collapse under the weight of such a big backpack.

'We'll work something out,' I repeat to myself.

Sunday, 1.25 a.m. Hélène disappears into an elegant building. The lobby and stairwell are finely wrought in a perfect imitation of yellow Sienna marble, and a thick carpet covers the stairs.

She pulls a huge keyring out of her bag and opens an imposing door on the first floor. The hallway is spacious, with several doors leading to the rest of the flat, which is laid out like a star. The décor inside is in stark contrast to that in the communal parts of the building. The collection of eclectic furniture, devoid of any stylistic coherence, has the air of a flea market. Worn Persian rugs cover the antique wooden floor, and futuristic-looking lamps infuse the rooms with soft light. The walls are all hidden by shelves filled with books and files. But strangely, as is often the case in such places, it somehow all fits together better than if it had been meticulously thought out. The atmosphere is no less soothing than if it had been professionally designed in a minimalist style.

The first room off to the side is a small office. A rather prim young man – he looks like the archetypal teacher's pet – is sitting calmly at his desk, his attention focused on his computer screen. Hélène interrupts him for an update. The new group is waiting for her. Two men and a woman arrived earlier in the evening, and he sent them off to where they were needed. She thanks her right-hand man and strides into the neighbouring room, which is much bigger.

A dozen people between the ages of thirty and eighty are having a friendly conversation around a wooden table in the middle of the room. They warmly welcome Hélène, who quickly asks how each of them is doing. Are they adapting well? Are they happy with their accommodation? Do they feel they have the required skills for their new jobs? Overall, everyone seems happy. Just one man, with a foreign accent, asks for individual rather than group sessions. She tells him to see Aurélien in the office to schedule an appointment.

Over the course of the next hour, each of them talks about their sleep, their work, and any difficulties they've had adapting to their new way of life. Hélène listens, offers advice and takes notes, then tells them she'll see them again next week.

She moves on to the next room. Sitting around a single table, small groups are huddled over books or notebooks in the white glow of the desk lamps. Bookcases cover every inch of wall space. One of the groups is engaged in an animated debate. Hélène makes her way towards them.

'These texts were written just to piss us off,' says a tall, skinny woman with long red hair, fine features and porcelain skin.

Hélène smiles and taps her on the shoulder. 'You should go home, Marianne, you're getting worked up. Miguel, how's your translation coming along?'

'I should finish it tomorrow. I spoke to the company on the phone today.'

'No other problems then? Everything's good?'

Philosophy teachers, schoolteachers, art lovers and people from all sorts of professional backgrounds gather here to study, discuss and write essays, which are sometimes published. Some of them come in whenever the mood strikes, stay for just a few hours a night, then go home. Others, like Marianne, a retired widow, have joined the Network full time and rarely leave.

Hélène finishes up in yet another room. A man with headphones is sitting at a keyboard, composing music on his computer. Another is lying on a sofa reading, while a woman dozes on a chaise longue, and a figure sits hunched over a notebook by the window. Ten people, all engaged in solitary activities, but together.

Hélène decides it's best not to bother them and makes her way back to Aurélien's desk to say goodbye. Outside, she nearly knocks over a woman who's on her way in. She's a former attendee from one of her insomnia groups, who's come for a first shy look at the Network. Hélène encourages her to go up and promises to check in on her tomorrow.

She carries on like this, going from neighbourhood to neighbourhood and building to building – each with varying levels of activity and noise, depending on what their occupants are working on. She makes sure the logistics are running smoothly, checks to see how everyone's work is coming along, and guides new arrivals. Each visit fills her with joy and pride at having accomplished her mission.

Monday, 2 a.m. Jacques is on his fourth round-trip to the basement in his building, carrying rubbish bags that are filled to the brim. He hopes the city's waste services will be understanding given the size of the pile. How many nights has it taken to reach this point? Each new bag he brings is a weight lifted off his shoulders.

Focused on the task at hand, Jacques doesn't notice the man who is watching him from the pavement across the road. Nor does he see him cross the road and approach him. He jumps when he feels a warm breath on his ear and hears a voice asking if he can take what he likes. Once he's overcome his fear, Jacques agrees – it's nothing but rubbish anyway. The homeless man rifles through the contents for a moment, then disappointedly selects a few pieces of fabric and two cushions.

'Everything's broken. Useless rubbish,' he says.

Before Jacques can reply, the man disappears around the corner with his meagre find. He's scared the shit out of the imposing psychiatrist, but he's spoken the truth. As if for the first time, Jacques realises the full extent of the destructive urge that has driven him to ruin all these things. He'd chosen to ignore it and soothe his conscience by telling himself that all the destruction had a purpose, that it was the only way to start again. That giving it away wouldn't have had the same effect . . .

At around three o'clock he closes the door to his flat, feeling a bit ashamed. He tries to forget the man as he paces the nearly empty space. His steps echo as if he were visiting the unoccupied flat with an estate agent. In his room he's kept the bed, the Ikea lamp and the alarm clock. He lies down without any hope of falling asleep. He thinks about his wife, who will never walk through the door again, then about Marie, who won't call him anymore, and about the patients he no longer wants to see. He momentarily contemplates taking all his sleeping pills at once.

Tuesday, 6 a.m. Lena has been lying awake in bed for an hour and a half. She's on her third reading of the letter she received from her father yesterday. Once a month he sends a letter that always says the same thing: *I want you and your brother to come live with me*. She studies the photos at length, hoping to find a detail, a clue. The tackily decorated flat, the palm trees, the beach, the bakery with her father posing proudly in front of it. The baby in the woman's arms. Why didn't he tell her? What came over him? He abandoned two children to go and have a third in the sun. There's no way she'll choose to waste away in that backward village. As if a snap of his fingers could fix everything – it was so typical of him. Lena would rather put up with her mother than have her father's new bimbo as a stepmother. That's her destiny, she realises – to live with her mother forever, since she'll never have enough money to rent a place of her own on a cleaner's salary. Maybe in the suburbs, eventually, but only over her dead body. Her head feels heavy. She struggles to sit up in bed, then pauses for a few seconds before standing. She totters to the bathroom – a seemingly endless journey on her weak legs. The drive that gets her out of bed every morning is beginning to dwindle. But Lena has to get out. She knows that outside, in the hours between night and dawn, is the only place where her anger will melt away.

6.30 a.m. She's about to apply her first touch of make-up, to hide the effects of lack of sleep on her face, when she hears a knocking on the door of the flat. The cat must be ramming his head into it. The sound picks up again, the rapping more urgent. It can't be the cat – even he isn't stupid enough to give himself a concussion. She hesitates. Who on earth could it be at this time of day? When she squints through the spy hole in the door she thinks she must be dreaming. The entire insomniacs' group is standing on the landing.

'What the hell are they doing here?' she mumbles as she reluctantly opens the door and watches them tiptoe inside. She stares at them, confused. Hervé looks like a giant in the small space. Jacques nervously clears his throat. Claire and Michèle seem to find the situation perfectly normal. Lena's mother suddenly emerges from her room – dressed and wearing a bit of make-up for the occasion. Much to her surprise, Lena realises her mother is still pretty when she makes a little effort. She could lose a few pounds, of course, but her skin is smooth, her features fine and her eyes, when she enhances them with a bit of eyeliner, are exceptionally beautiful. The older woman nods knowingly to her guests, then disappears into the kitchen.

Michèle, who seems to have instigated the initiative, speaks first. She seems to be in good spirits this morning – her eyes haven't shone so brightly in quite a while.

'Hélène gave us your phone number and address. We're here to help you study. With your mother's blessing, of course. Maybe we won't all be cured of insomnia any time soon, but as for you, my dear, you're going to get your diploma – I promise.'

Lena wonders what they stand to gain from this. She doesn't move a muscle. Annoyed at being forced to stay in, she keeps thinking of ways to get rid of them. But she's never been quick on her feet and her mother has already invited the group to sit down at the kitchen table.

'How exactly are you planning to go about this?' asks Lena from the doorway.

'We'll come over one morning a week until your exams,' replies Michèle. 'Here's a schedule.'

'It's our new sleep schedule. Let's hope it's more effective,' jokes Claire.

'As a former teacher I thought it might be a good idea to have a chat with your headmistress,' Michèle continues. 'She seems to have taken a real liking to you. We have the list of subjects you need to focus on. There's still hope. Each of us will help out with the subjects we know best.'

'I can help with figures,' offers Hervé.

Lena glances inquisitively at Jacques.

'He really wanted to come,' explains Claire. 'For moral support. As for me, I'm fluent in Spanish. That could come in handy for your international career.'

Lena's mother serves the coffee alongside a mountain of almond biscuits she made yesterday. Her daughter can hardly believe it as her mother hasn't baked a single thing since her husband left. Her mother takes her leave afterwards, followed by Jacques, who barely fits in the tiny kitchen.

Lena gives in and retrieves her backpack from the hallway. She peeks into the lounge, where she sees Jacques and her mother sitting side by side on the sofa, glued to the morning television shows. 'Ridiculous,' mumbles Lena, who finds their closeness disturbing. She might as well jump on top of him while she's at it she thinks. François, who can tell something unusual is going on, comes out of his room to hide under the kitchen table, where Michèle slips him a steady supply of biscuits with a warm smile.

Over the course of an hour, Michèle calls upon her talents as a good listener and excellent teacher – as fervent about this new mission as she is about her prayers. Hervé, who's usually so quiet, surprises Lena with his ability to make himself understood. Though she's quiet for the moment, Claire is meticulously preparing Spanish worksheets for her new student. Jacques pops in only to fill his plate with biscuits and pour himself another cup of coffee. Despite all her efforts to concentrate, Lena is exhausted at the idea of doing this again. She bluntly tells her newfound tutors that it's no use, that there's no point in going back.

'I never gave up on a single student during my career,' Michèle affirms proudly. 'I hope you'll forgive my lack of humility, but even the most hopeless cases succeeded thanks to me.'

Claire and Hervé nod enthusiastically and Lena realises there's nothing more to say. And just as they came in – quietly, one after another – they go, leaving her feeling thoughtful as she sits surrounded by her notes. Her mother has gone back to bed and probably won't come out for the rest of the day. *Why not accept their help since they've offered?* Lena feels so calm. In fact, during their study session, she felt something she hasn't felt since her father left: safe.

'François, come out from under the table,' she orders. 'I'll make your breakfast, but then I have to get to Franck's.'

The little boy, who's enjoyed the lesson as much as she has, emerges from his hiding place.

7.30 a.m. The air outside is almost warm. The streetlights shine on the wet pavement. Lena takes a deep breath. For once her legs aren't shaking as she walks in a state of near euphoria. She crosses the street to reach the café, ignoring the red light on the pedestrian crossing – and the approaching car. She doesn't see it coming.

Distant voices keep her conscious for a few moments. Then there's nothing but silence, emptiness and darkness.

Wednesday, 1.30 a.m. I see him sitting at the back of the café. His eyes are closed, and his wine glass is half-full alongside a nearly empty bottle. Most of the customers are gathered at the bar. I can feel their eyes on me. They must find it a source of huge amusement: a strange woman coming to find the solitary regular. When I get closer, Hervé seems to be able to feel my presence and opens his eyes. His face comes to life. He didn't shave for his interview and his dutifully filled-out sleep log is sitting on the table.

'Have you found a job?' I ask, drinking from his glass.

'My social worker told me to apply for a position as a security guard. I have my second interview tomorrow.'

'You must be joking,' I say, incredulously.

'It's for a retirement home. No need for muscles.'

'They need security guards in retirement homes?'

'They're needed everywhere these days. But it's mostly to make sure the residents don't escape.'

He looks so troubled that I stifle my urge to laugh. It's obviously a sensitive subject so I decide to steer clear of it. He seems in a hurry to leave anyway – he's already wearing his coat. As soon as he finishes his wine, we stand up and go.

At last, it's feeling warmer outside. The arrival of spring is comforting. Ahead of me, Hervé has already begun walking at a swift pace on his long legs. I'd like to ask him to slow down and wait for me, or even take his arm, but I run to catch up instead. We spend the evening much like last time, but it's a new route this time, with buildings we've never seen before. We hang back and meticulously trail Hélène for two hours. I suggest to Hervé that we should confront her here and now, but he doesn't want to. Not yet. He'd rather find out more first. I don't understand why he's so reluctant, but don't want to upset him. I warn him he won't get me to tag along for a third time, though. I may be an insomniac, but that doesn't mean I have the energy to waste on endless nocturnal hikes – even though the situation really does intrigue me. Hélène, who has always seemed so utterly predictable, is clearly leading a double life.

On my suggestion this time, we go back to his little flat for a steaming cup of coffee after we're done. We savour it in silence. It's strange how much at home I feel here despite the uninviting décor.

Hervé sits at the foot of the bed, in the same position as last time, while I try to get comfortable on the old sofa. He suggests that I might want to lie down on the bed, explaining that it's more comfortable and that he doesn't want me to hurt my back. It would be a bold offer in most circumstances, but nothing here seems suspicious. He hands me a pillow. I ask him if two insomniacs together add up to one good sleeper. He bursts into a hearty laugh I've never heard from him before, but then stops short, as if he's made some sort of faux pas. We both end up lying there, fully dressed, without speaking for a while.

'Are you planning to go home?' he finally asks.

'I don't think so,' I reply simply.

'Ah. How's work?'

'I've got back into it.'

'That's good. It's important not to fall too far behind.'

'Duly noted. Are you going to go to sleep?'

'You first – go ahead.'

'All right. Thanks. Goodnight, detective.'

I can feel Hervé smile in the darkness. A gentle warmth radiates from the centre of my being – from exactly the same place where a dull pain usually reminds me that I'm all alone.

When I wake, there's a note on the table again. *I'm at my interview. I've left you my spare key in case you need a quiet place to work.*

I go to the kitchen to make myself some coffee. When I open the window, I'm surprised to find a comprehensive collection of herbs growing in pots hanging all around it. When I return to the lounge, it's bathed in light. The bed, striped with beams of sunlight, beckons me. I immediately fall into a deep sleep. When I wake up again, it's after noon and I have the unfamiliar feeling of being well-rested.

9

Monday, 7.40 a.m. Hélène is in the middle of a phone call, which she draws to a close when she sees me coming. Hervé and I have agreed that today is the day we'll shed some light on her nocturnal activities. She gives me a surprised look – I don't usually turn up early – and then welcomes me warmly. Just as I'm about to make the most of our time alone to start my questioning, Jacques and Michèle walk in. They look like they haven't slept a wink. Michèle, who had come back to life at Lena's last week, is now deathly pale again. Next, Hervé comes in looking like a frightened animal. Why has everyone decided to be on time today? In the end, Hélène starts the session before I get my chance.

'For this last meeting, I'd like to take the time to go over the results each of you have achieved. And then I'd like to talk to you about an alternative.'

I seize the opportunity she doesn't realise she's just given me. 'Might this alternative have something to do with your nightly outings?' I ask.

Hélène is caught off-guard, but it doesn't throw her. 'You know about that? You've heard of the Network?' she replies.

'What network? No. Hervé and I just crossed paths with you one night.'

'Well, why didn't you come and ask me about it?'

I'm a little taken aback by her lack of embarrassment. 'You seemed to be on some sort of special, mysterious mission and we didn't want to interrupt.'

'There's nothing mysterious about it. I just didn't want to talk about it too soon, that's all,' she claims bluntly.

'I'm not sure I understand,' says Jacques. 'You're saying that Hélène here, our sleep specialist, doesn't sleep?'

'That's right, doctor. Small world, isn't it? Since you're an insomniac psychiatrist. But you're right, it is pretty incredible,' I reply.

'It's true,' Hélène adds calmly. 'I don't sleep much. Not much at all . . . Yes, I suppose I'm an insomniac.'

'You too?' mumbles Michèle. Her shoulders slump, and her face crumples. The light at the end of her dark tunnel has just gone out.

'Can you tell us more?' I insist.

'Of course, detective. At night I work as a psychologist for a unique network. I'm also its president!'

'What's this now?' Jacques asks disinterestedly, as if nothing could ever surprise him.

'Something truly unusual, which might interest some of you. Let me explain. So, five years ago, a man named Théodore Orian took part in the same sessions we are having. (Unfortunately, he died six months ago at the age of ninety.) He was a very educated and very wealthy man – you'll see why this matters soon. He was a neurological research scientist and a well-known philosopher – it's easy to find his essays in any bookshop if you're interested. But I'm losing the thread. Not long after our meetings, when he realised that sleep restriction hadn't worked for him, he got in touch with me and we entered into a serious debate about the difficulties insomniacs face. At a time when society has all sorts of groups, for special interests and even specific disorders, insomnia remains a solitary condition. He had an idea to change all that and he needed my help to do it. The Orian Network is the result of our partnership.'

'What did he die of?' interrupts Hervé.

'A heart attack.'

Suddenly panicked, he places his hand on his heart. To help him calm down, I place my own on his arm.

Hélène tightens her grip on her steaming cup of coffee, then continues her story. 'Théodore had two theories. First, that chronic insomniacs like yourselves – don't worry, you'll see that's not necessarily such a terrible thing – can only express themselves at night. And I don't just mean in terms of artistic creativity. Think about it. Michèle at the church, Hervé on his nocturnal adventures, Lena and her early-morning visits to the café. It's as if something were pulling you elsewhere, as if the night has more to offer than the daytime ever will.'

'That's taking things a bit far, don't you think, Hélène? You're supposed to help us with our insomnia, not sell us the positive aspects of staying up all night!' Jacques chimes in resentfully. 'I see plenty of grieving or traumatised patients who slept like babies before their lives were shaken to the core.'

But Hélène continues, impervious to his criticism. 'Theodore felt that night time is the best time for communing with your inner voice. But this precious voice is drowned out by anxiety, fear and anger about not being able to function well during the day like everyone else. And perhaps the people you mention, Jacques, may only be able to talk about painful things, and express their suffering, at nights, and somewhere where they're not alone. There's no time or space for that sort of thing during the day! You know what society is like these days. Everything has to be fast and profitable, whatever the cost,' Hélène explains passionately.

'Maybe, but all this talk of inner voices is a bit too esoteric to be taken seriously—'

'Jacques,' interrupts Michèle, 'If you intend to keep that up, you can leave! I'm interested in hearing what she has to say!'

We all turn towards Michèle, whose sudden authoritativeness comes as a surprise. An instinctive reflex from her time as a teacher, I suppose.

'Please continue, Hélène,' she says.

'Théodore also believed that this subset of insomniacs doesn't really want to go back to sleeping normally. I know it might sound crazy, but try not to react without really thinking it through. His theory was that they don't realise this until they're freed of the obligations imposed on them by society. So, he wanted – and could afford– to create a community where insomniacs would feel at home. Somewhere they could work, create, talk, write – whatever – without having to be alone with their existential anxiety, doubts and fears. Somewhere they could do everything they were unable to do during the day, after a sleepless night.'

Hélène stops long enough to take a few sips of her coffee and sees that we're all hanging on her every word.

'The second theory is that insomnia may be the consequence of an unmet need – perhaps something as simple as a lack of safety or affection. People often turn up at the Network relatively early in the night – not everyone is brave enough to get out of bed in the early hours of the morning – and get comfortable in one of the rooms, where they take part in a group discussion or simply savour a cup of herbal tea. Just knowing they're surrounded by others like them is soothing. Before long, they stop coming, or come in only now and again. Just knowing that the place is there and open to them is enough to get them sleeping again. Everyone uses the Network as he or she sees fit. We adapt things to suit their needs, using our knowledge and infrastructure to support them. The only rules are mutual respect and kindness. People from all different backgrounds come together and get to know one another. At the Network, there are no labels for gender, religion, socio-economic status or profession.'

'That sounds a bit too good to be true, doesn't it?' I venture.

'It's not, Claire, because it works!' counters Hélène. 'And from a purely medical perspective, Théodore was perfectly aware that the human body is unable to adapt to this inverted circadian rhythm.'

'There are plenty of night workers,' objects Hervé.

'True, but many studies have shown that the rate of illness and depression is high among them. I helped him turn his ideas into a reality. A sustainable, long-term project.'

'And all of that happens in the buildings we saw you visit?' I ask.

'Yes, Théodore owned about twenty of them in neighbouring areas. They were mostly rented out to doctors' surgeries, barristers, consultancies and such. I don't know how he did it – I prefer not to know such things – but once he'd decided to create the Network, he was able to persuade everyone who was there to leave. Each building now has sound-proof rooms, for people who decide to stay for a while, large kitchens, study rooms, lounges and more. We've even started to develop the concept abroad.'

Hélène pauses to let us digest what she's said. This time no one speaks. We've just learned about the existence of a hitherto unimaginable world – a world specially designed for us. I look around the room and realise we're all having a hard time believing it.

After a few moments of silence, Hélène continues. 'We're still in the early stages, of course. The Network has only been operational for four years. Théodore wanted to give insomniacs whose lives have become too difficult a haven – somewhere outside their homes – where they feel safe. And that's what I'm trying to create.'

'So, what exactly goes on there?' I ask, unconvinced.

'For the moment, a lot of different experiments. We're testing this new way of life every day. It's complex, but we're very organised.'

'What kind of experiments?'

'Nothing terrible, Claire – don't look at me like that. Light therapy, for example. We've fitted all the Network buildings with lamps that emit a light that's almost as intense as the rays of the sun, to minimise the negative effects of being awake in the dark.'

'And this community is open to all insomniacs?' Michèle asks hopefully. 'Even retired people?'

'It all depends on the amount of time you spend there. But, in theory, if your insomnia has become too much for you to handle alone, that's when I intervene. I often select people at the end of these sessions. As for seniors, Michèle, as long as they're in good health, as I'm sure you are, they are more than welcome. There are already quite a few of them at the Network. They often have talents linked to their former professions or to an interest that they can share. And they're generally active participants. If their pensions aren't generous enough to pay their dues, our means-based economic scheme helps make up the difference.'

'So we're basically your guinea pigs.'

'No, Jacques. But, if at the end of these sessions, you haven't got the results you wanted, the Network is another possible solution.'

'What about insomniacs who don't live in the city?' I ask, thinking of the village I used to live in.

'I wish I could welcome everyone, but the Network has its limits, and geographical restrictions are among them. That said, we have implemented a hotline. It's not the same, I know, but every night volunteers take calls from insomniacs who can't join us physically. We've even started using Skype for group sessions. It's a little strange at first, but you get used to it quickly and eventually forget the screen. Since you live farther out, Claire, it might be a nice option for you.'

Hervé gives me a knowing glance. I stare at my feet. Hélène

obviously doesn't know about my new living arrangements at the hotel.

Everyone at the table seems to be lost in thought.

'So it's kind of like a secret society?' I joke.

Hélène smiles. 'No. Though it's true we don't advertise to the general public. If we hung posters in the Métro, we'd be overrun with applications. And I'm afraid not all of the people who contacted us would be insomniacs. We ask our members to sign confidentiality agreements. Word of mouth could have a negative impact. Healthcare specialists know about us, and I'm constantly working with sleep specialists from all of the city's hospitals. They are the only ones authorised to send us new applicants. That said, we're flexible. For example, if one of you had a chronic insomniac among your loved ones, we wouldn't turn them away. But they'd have to take some tests, be interviewed, and participate in group therapy first. Our numbers are growing every day. Luckily, Théodore planned ahead, and there are still several empty buildings. And, as I said, there are only about fifteen permanent residents. The others come and go.'

'Permanent residents?'

'Yes, Michèle. People like Aurélien, my right-hand man, who also happens to be Théodore's grandson, both live in and work for the Network. There's Marianne, a philosophy professor who's writing a manifesto; Lucas, a former electrician who works as our building manager; Laurence, a psychologist, and a few more. Everyone else stays for a short while or only ever comes in for a night here and there. In the group I had just before yours, there was a new mother, who had already been an insomniac while pregnant, but got worse after the birth of her baby. The baby cried all the time, so sleep was out of the question anyway. She turned up one night, with the baby snuggled into a sling on her chest. I admit I was sceptical. Her husband wasn't particularly supportive, and the loneliness was too much for her. But I made her comfortable in a quiet room, surrounded by a few people talking softly, and she fell asleep straight away. She and her baby slept for five straight hours. She came back regularly for a while, then began spacing out her visits. Her time with us gave her back the confidence and comfort she needed.

'What about those who live within the . . . Network, as you call it. Do they sleep during the day?' asks Hervé.

'To cut a long story short, each insomniac benefits from individual monitoring to get a clear picture of their sleep needs. We've noticed that, following a productive period of completing fulfilling tasks, they fall into a deep sleep around the middle of the night.'

'Could you give us a concrete example?' asks the former accountant.

Hélène stands up, her body expressing her impatience though her voice stays perfectly level. 'Let's say it's after midnight, so you think there's no chance of getting enough sleep since your alarm is set for 6.30 a.m. Well, imagine what it would be like if you were in a warm and welcoming place where everyone else was in the same situation. You could join a discussion group, work in a study room to catch up, sleep in a relaxing bedroom, or talk to a doctor. And all that without the fear of the alarm going off in the morning. One of our goals is to help our members keep their jobs or find a new one that allows them to work from home? It's the most diffi-cult piece of the puzzle, since it simply doesn't work for certain professions, and quite a few companies are unwilling to try it out. But our list of cooperative companies is growing. Sometimes the Network itself hires people, too, such as psychologists, osteopaths and accountants. You get the idea. Let's say Hervé decides to join. He could work for us directly and choose to live full-time at the Network or keep his current

flat. It's important that members remain financially indepen-
dent if possible, if only to pay their dues. Though we have a
significant endowment, of course, without which none of this
would be possible.'

'So, joining isn't turning your back on a normal life?' I ask.

'What's a normal life? Every night I see people who have
made peace with themselves by turning the wakefulness they
used to see as a curse into an enjoyable experience that is
only possible at night. And, as I've said several times, the
Network is just a step, a transition. It's not an end in and of
itself. It's not a paradise, either. We accommodate members
with different backgrounds and difficulties. There are tensions,
problems to be managed and disagreements, from time to
time. Members often need psychological support, but no
more than elsewhere, really. You're all very welcome to come
and see for yourselves.'

I check the time, which seems to have flown for once.

'If Lena were here, she'd say it sounds like a zombie cult,'
I joke. 'Talking of which, where is she? Have you heard
from her?'

'Ah, yes, I meant to bring that up at the beginning of the
session,' says Hélène as she sits back down and takes off her
glasses to rub her eyes. She's focusing on choosing her words
carefully. It's obvious something has happened.

'Is she all right?' Michèle asks worriedly.

'I won't beat around the bush. There was an accident. She
was hit by a car. She's in a coma. The doctors can't say how
things will turn out.'

Michèle places her hand in front of her mouth to stifle a
gasp.

'Poor girl,' mumbles Hervé.

'How did it happen?' I ask.

'It was one morning last week,' Hélène explains. She hesitates, then continues. 'Right after your visit. It happened just

outside the café where she spends all her time. She crossed the road when the pedestrian crossing light was red, without even checking for cars. I'm so sorry to have to be the one to tell you.'

We're all shocked. I want to scream. If she hadn't been so tired, maybe she would have looked both ways. She was so weak. This accident feels like a failure for all of us. It reveals just how terrible insomnia can be. And what about her diploma? No hope of that now. That was her ticket to a better life. The sound of my rage-filled fist pounding into the table makes everyone jump.

Even though the session has run over time, none of us seems inclined to leave. Michèle is silent, a haggard look on her face. Jacques hasn't opened his eyes since Hélène shared the news; his face remains hidden in his hands.

'So this is our last meeting?' asks Hervé nervously.

'We'll still be in touch. I'll send each of you a written assessment by email,' Hélène says reassuringly. 'I'll give you precise instructions to follow if you want to continue with the method. Michèle, I'd like to talk to you before you go. And you're all welcome at one o'clock tonight at the Network's headquarters. I know this is difficult, but that just makes it even more important for all of you to be there.'

Monday, 11.30 p.m. In the hospital corridor that leads to Lena's room, we come across a sobbing man with tattooed arms. Jacques stops and gently taps him on the shoulder, as if they know one another. Without a second thought, the man throws himself into Jacques's arms. Surprised, we give them their space. 'The café owner, Lena's friend,' whispers Jacques, who, clearly embarrassed by the situation, tries to wriggle free of the man's embrace.

The room is dimly lit by a neon ceiling light over the bed.

If it weren't for the bandages wrapped around her head and the bruise on her cheek, I would have thought Lena was sleeping peacefully. Her mother, who's been drowning her pain in high doses of antidepressants, welcomes us without letting go of her daughter's hand. François is fast asleep on a mattress on the floor next to the bed. We sit down, all except for Jacques, who remains standing next to the window attentively watching the comings and goings in the car park below. Half an hour later, Hervé has dozed off, his long legs resting on the foot of the bed. Michèle's lips move in silence as she continues an intense internal dialogue.

I stare at Lena's face and at her emaciated frame beneath the sheets. The tubes and mask. I start to wonder if she's not better off here, rather than fighting invisible forces that always win. An absent father, an unfit mother, poverty, loneliness. And then I realise I'm thinking of myself. Lena still has her life ahead of her. I turn my gaze to Hervé. Watching him sleep soothes me, as does this room. I've always found hospitals reassuring and never miss a chance to visit them. Two years ago, my grandmother spent the last weeks of her life in a room like this one, and I was the only member of the family to spend several hours a week by her side. No one really wanted to see off the cold, manipulative old woman. Not even her children. As for me, I enjoyed strolling from the cafeteria to her room and from her room to the vending machine, chatting with the nurses and a few older patients who were still full of life. I felt at home. One night, she drew her last breath and expired with a sarcastic laugh. I was holding her hand. After that, I had to leave the room to make way for what came next. I still remember how I listened to the noises in the corridor as they petered out at night, until only the occasional sound of a lone trolley or a fit of laughter from a faraway group of nurses would reach me.

I take Hervé's notebook out of my bag. I've got into the

habit of jotting ideas down in it whenever they come to mind.

Jacques finally turns away from the window and breaks the silence, as if he's found a solution. 'So, shall we go and check out this paradise for insomniacs?' he asks.

I stretch out, trying to wake up my sore muscles. Let's go. It may sound too good to be true, but, still, it's reassuring to at least be able to imagine that such a place exists. A place right here in the city where nights would no longer be a nightmare.

I gently place my hand on Hervé's shoulder, but he jumps anyway. Each of us kisses Lena's head before leaving. Michèle draws the sign of a cross on the girl's forehead as silent tears stream down her cheeks. Then she kneels down next to the sleeping little boy on the mattress. Her face is as pale as a ghost's. I must make sure Jacques or Hélène looks after her now that our meetings are over. We can't just abandon her. Maybe Jacques could prescribe something, at least. Lena's mother is talking to the psychiatrist, her hands on her face as she shakes her head. He gives her his card and offers to help.

We all promise to come back tomorrow and every day after. With heavy hearts, we leave Lena behind. Though none of us will admit it, we're all terrified the night will take her from us. We leave arm in arm, headed for our second appointment of the night, unable to return to the solitude of our separate rooms.

10

Eight months later

Monday, 1.00 a.m. The last patient has just left. Lots of people love the idea of seeing a psychiatrist in the middle of the night – Jacques's waiting list is proof of that. When people type 'after-hours psychiatrist' in their search engine, he pops up near the top of the list, right after SOS Psychiatrist and online-psych.com. A niche market just waiting to be discovered. He stays at his desk for a moment to finish his notes. His clothes clash starkly with the strictly minimalist décor around him – his cashmere jumpers are the only trace of his former life. Jacques turns out the lights without listening to the messages on his flashing telephone. It's probably his daughter trying once again to convince him to join them for Christmas. He claims he has a seminar to attend. He just can't bear it this year. He doesn't want to have to pretend anymore. He'll see his children later. He's even thinking of going to see his grandson in the yurt in the middle of nowhere.

1.30 a.m. At the same time every night, he returns to his studio flat, just behind the door at the far end of his office, and falls asleep within seconds. Something strange happened when the meetings ended and he moved out of his old flat:

he suddenly started following Hélène's guidelines to the letter. He used to constantly mock them, but from that day onwards he began taking them seriously – he even filled out his sleep log every day, to get an idea of his progress. And, miraculously, after a few weeks, it worked. He slept without a single pill. Ever since, he's been incredibly strict. He no longer goes out but lives like a hermit on the other side of the city, far from his former life in every sense of the word. With the money from the sale of his flat, he made a generous donation to the Network, though it was less out of altruism than to make himself feel better. He still feels so guilty about Marie. And ashamed. Ashamed that he didn't even try with the group, that he single-handedly destroyed all his former things, which were worth a lot of money, that he crossed the red line. A mistake he still can't forgive himself for.

Two days after he handed Lena's mother his card at the hospital, she rang his doorbell. Jacques didn't think she would use it at all, much less dare to turn up unannounced. It was early evening. She asked him for help. She had to hold on, for her children. Jacques awkwardly explained that he was too involved in her life to have the neutrality and objectivity required, but offered to recommend a colleague instead. He apologised – he should have thought of that before giving her his business card. Sitting on what was left of the sofa in his office, she insisted, offering up all sorts of arguments. Jacques realised the woman must have a very strong personality when she wasn't numbed by medication. Finally, faced with his categorical refusal, she went quiet.

The room was silent for a long while. Her mascara had left black lines streaming down her cheeks. She calmly asked for a drink of something strong before leaving. He noticed her dress – plain but with a low neckline. He refused again. Just one glass, she pleaded. She needed it, given the circumstances. He hesitated, mostly because of the cocktail of drugs she was on. Then, out of weakness, he took out a bottle of whisky. They had a glass, then two, and after that he's not sure. She initiated things, standing up to take his hand, and Jacques let her. Her desire was so strong it was hard to resist. Her heavy breasts, the scent of jasmine in her hair, her wide hips, full thighs, olive skin . . . Jacques suddenly wanted her. He could only remember Catherine's thin frame, and a few other young, angular bodies he'd had brief affairs with. And, though he was ashamed to admit it, this woman's despair and her need to be loved fuelled his desire.

Afterwards, lying on the floor, he didn't know what to say or do. He didn't make a single kind gesture – nothing. He felt awkward, already disgusted with himself for taking advantage of a woman who was having such a hard time. She got dressed with her back to him, then left without a word.

When Jacques returned to Lena's hospital room alone a week later, he mumbled excuses. 'I'm sorry, I shouldn't have. I regret it.' Lena's mother stood tall and proud right in front of him. Her breasts nearly touched the buttons on his shirt. He'd never seen a look so full of disappointment and disdain. 'Well I don't,' she replied defiantly. And then she left. Ever since, whenever he comes to visit Lena, she goes out for a walk. Jacques also cut his ties with the group, before they could do it themselves. He's happy enough with his very reduced social life.

Sometimes he refers patients to Hélène – it's up to her to decide how to manage them. She's his only link to the Network. Since he's lowered his rate and changed neighbourhoods, he has new patients with more modest incomes. It reminds him of the early part of his career. He finally feels like he's useful again.

At one o'clock every night Jacques turns off his light, his mobile and his computer, then falls asleep, exhausted by his five hours of sessions with patients. Sometimes, before dozing off, when he can no longer control the images coming from his brain, he sees that magnificently voluptuous body hovering over him.

Tuesday, 11.45 a.m. Michèle knows she won't fall asleep tonight, but that's OK. She gets up, gets dressed, and calls a taxi to meet up with Hélène. There's always something to be done – arranging housing for new residents, listing companies to negotiate working from home with, scheduling group sessions, welcoming drop-in insomniacs, and more. She moves from floor to floor, smiling at faces that have become familiar to her. Sometimes she joins in discussion groups or shares her detailed knowledge of theology. Her open mind and remarkable kindness always calm people down when tensions mount in a debate. She also occasionally sits in a reading room to enjoy the silent company of the other occupants. Hélène often finds Michèle sleeping on the sofa in the early morning hours.

She's been sleeping better of late, though insomnia still punctuates many of her nights. When it rears its head, she makes her way to the Network, which has become a home from home. Though she would have liked to, she wasn't able to join immediately. She first had to go to a sleep rehab centre and agree to treatment with a psychiatrist at the hospital, whom she continues to see today. After Lena's accident, Michèle's husband was so disturbed by her condition that he almost had her committed. She was overwhelmed by her hallucinations and could easily have fallen permanently into her imaginary world.

3 a.m. When she gets home she sits down next to the sleeping child without even taking off her coat. She's exhausted, but wants to marvel at the view, which moves her to tears every night. She runs her hand through his thick black hair, unable to believe he's really there. *Sweet boy. Life hasn't been easy for you, so far.*

Michèle's patience is limitless as she tries to calm the boy's daily temper tantrums and tears. She'd like to watch over him until morning, but her husband peeks his sleepy head into the room. Time for bed. Michèle stands up reluctantly, drawing a cross on the boy's smooth forehead, just as she does on his sister's every time she visits her in the hospital. *Sweet dreams, François.*

When she got home from rehab, Michèle went to visit Lena's mother at the hospital every day. François was always there, too worked up to stay in one place in the tiny room. Michèle couldn't bear the thought of keeping the poor boy inside all the time and gradually encouraged his mother to let her take him out – first to the cafeteria for an ice cream, then to a restaurant for lunch, gradually progressing to trips to the cinema, and walks in the park. She had to be careful not to come on too strong, but in the end the boy's mother was clearly relieved to see her child in good hands. After a few weeks, with no explicit agreement between either adult, François began staying with Michèle, who was unbelievably happy to have a child at home. A mother without children and a child in need of a mother – it was a perfect fit and together they built a deep but still fragile bond. Every now and again, Michèle still goes to the church at night. Her life now includes a living, breathing child, but in the darkness, she still lights candles for the ones she never got to meet. Before heading to her bedroom, Michèle goes to the lounge to turn off the lights on the Christmas tree. It's the first tree they've had since her first miscarriage. This year Christmas will be joyful again.

Wednesday, 10 p.m. It's time. Lena hears a gentle knock on the door. They say hello to her mother, then come in quietly, sitting in their usual places. They arrive together, except for Jacques, who visits once a week during the day. Such an idiot, cutting off ties like that. Claire always chooses the armchair tucked away in the corner. Hervé opts for a chair, propping his long legs up on the foot of the bed. Michèle sits across from Lena's mother, who spends every day by her daughter's side. Her depression seems to get worse every day. Lena can't help but feel as if her mother's finally found a good excuse for the state she's in. She's put on more weight and doesn't bother with make-up anymore. In retrospect, Lena liked it better when she dressed like a flirt in the bakery. Luckily, her father has agreed to pay the rent for the flat. Without his help, she'd probably be living on the street.

The whispering begins. As if they might wake her by speaking normally. Today they've brought little gifts, which they leave on the bedside table, and Claire hangs fairy lights over the bed. At first they came every night. Then, with the Network, life went on, and they had less time. But they never miss a Tuesday night visit. Since he knows she'll have company, it's the only night of the week when Franck allows himself a break. The poor bartender has had to hire a part-time waiter so that he can visit Lena for a few hours every day.

They seem to be doing better. Even Claire. And the Network is intriguing. They talk about it enthusiastically – especially Hervé and Michèle, who apparently often run into each other there at night. Maybe I can convince Jacques to go when I wake up, thinks Lena.

In the hushed silence of the room where the only thing that changes is the shade of the light from outside, Lena feels like she's in a cocoon, which a breathless sob pierces several times a day. She can hear it in her deep sleep. *Just let me rest a while longer, Mum. I promise I'll wake up soon*, she thinks, hoping her mother can hear her too.

It will take a little more strength than she has at the moment to leave this delightful, pain-numbing sleep. No more nausea, anger or disappointment. Just divine rest. It's going to take some serious motivation to leave it behind.

Thursday, 2:10 a.m. Hervé is sitting at his desk, across from Aurélien's, in the small room next to the hallway. Thanks to the Network, he didn't have to take that job as a security guard. But the silence that reigned between he and Aurélien on Hervé's first night here didn't augur well for their professional relationship. They both suffered from severe shyness. Hervé, who couldn't stand it anymore, finally broke the silence on the third night.

'I'm sorry if Hélène didn't give you any choice but to share this space with me. She offered me another office, but I thought . . .'

'I understand. Do you want to leave?' asked Aurélien nervously.

'No, not at all, but if you . . .' replied Hervé awkwardly.

'Stay, then, if I don't bother you.'

And that was that. Since then, the pair come together every night like a couple of old friends. They're too scrupulous to spend their time chatting during work hours, but they share glances and offer discreet signs of affection. Hervé and Aurélien manage the Network's accounts – debts, rents, donations, loans and salaries. It's much more complicated than an ad campaign, but Hervé has regained his talent for numbers now that he can sleep late in the morning. And nap.

3 a.m. He turns off his computer. He'll work more in the afternoon, while Claire's correcting proofs. The time they spend together in silence at the dining table is one of his favourite moments of the day. He's always eager to get home, secretly hoping that she'll still be awake. Sometimes she waits for him in the dark lounge with only the glow from the lamp on the bedside table – the dim light makes him think of a theatre set. Her tired eyes look up at him and she smiles. He tells her all about his night as he undresses to join her. She listens attentively but always falls asleep before he's finished, her book open on her chest, giving Hervé the opportunity to contemplate her face at length. His greatest pleasure in life is watching Claire fall asleep, and now, watching her as her belly grows round. He didn't have to push too hard. At first she said she was too old. A baby at forty wasn't a good idea. She could die in childbirth and would be an old mother in any case. And where would they even put the baby? He quickly brushed aside her doubts. Then she met his gaze in silence, a strange look on her face, and without warning, burst into tears in his arms, her sobbing interspersed with incomprehensible phrases. He didn't try to console her with words – he just held her, surprised at first and then relieved that she was finally letting go of so many years of shame and rage.

Two months later he shouted with joy and she with panic. The test was positive. To calm her down he had to promise on his grown-up son's life that if she didn't feel she could love the baby, he would love him or her enough for both of them.

Friday, 5 a.m. Before getting out of bed I listen to Hervé's regular breathing and study the slight movements of his face. Then I get up and quietly make my way to the kitchen. Both of us cherish the other's sleep. I like knowing he's fast asleep and, to keep from waking him, I set up a little corner near the window with a folding desk. I come here whenever I wake up early or can't sleep.

I turn on the coffee maker and my computer. I'm on my last proof of the Network's economic model – the final document in a detailed presentation of the organisation. Hélène needs to send it to a similar group in London today.

I don't sleep any more than before, but the nights are no longer filled with malevolent forces that continue to plague me in the daylight hours. And I don't panic at the first signs of a sleepless night anymore. If I can't sleep, I wait patiently for Hervé to come home from the Network.

The first time I went there that night with the others I liked the place right away. It felt like a charming boarding-house. There was always someone in the corridor, someone talking in the kitchen, libraries to hide away in, comfortable bedrooms that were just about soundproofed enough to dull the sound from the neighbouring rooms into a reassuring murmur. For several weeks, I spent a few hours there every night. Hervé and I would leave our flat together at around nine o'clock. I would go to a study room or help Michèle, but I often ended up falling asleep in a corner. Hélène offered me a job and a desk, but I quickly realised that I preferred working from home. I'm happy the Network exists to give people like me a new lease of life, but I don't think commu-nity living is for me. You can't completely change who you are. Hervé is enough to reassure me, all on his own. He's made a few friends, who come over for dinner now and again. That's more than enough of a social life for me.

A cookbook by a Michelin-starred pastry chef is sitting on the tiny work surface, open at a page featuring an extremely complicated cake. Hervé has big plans for his son's birthday tonight. He's scribbled a grocery list on a Post-it. He's been asking me for gift ideas for a week already. I gently suggested that an envelope of money wasn't the most personal choice. I sit down and rub my belly in circles, as if trying to soothe something inside. Or maybe to soothe myself. It's almost Christmas but, strangely, I don't feel the least bit depressed. In fact, I'm looking forward to celebrating with Hervé and his son.

There's a tiny Christmas tree in the corner of the lounge and a few strands of fairy lights on the walls. And yet, meagre though they are, these decorations bring me more joy than the magnificent tree of the big stone house I shared with Paul, which now seems light years away.

I spend quite some time watching the sky change colours as I drink my coffee. I'd better get on with things though – the day will be over in a flash. It's Wednesday, my day with François. I take him to lunch and then to the hospital to see Lena; afterwards, we go to the cinema or to a park depending on the weather and his preference. Then I drop him back at Michèle's – and we can't be late for dinner. I often spend the evening there, too, and if Michèle decides to go to the Network, I sometimes go with her.

I gently tap the keys with my fingers to pass the time, then take a deep breath, as if I'm about to dive off the high board, and open a new file. I stare at the blank page on my screen until I can see nothing but thousands of tiny dots of light.

Hervé has been mentioning it for months, patiently encouraging me, but I always find a good excuse – there's too much proofing work, I'm too tired, and it's not as if I have anything interesting to say. 'Write about your nights,' he always says. 'Our nights, the nights of all us who can't sleep.'

Acknowledgements

Thank you to Catherine, Élodie, Dominique, Jean, Couetsch and Arnaud for sharing your nights of insomnia with me. Thank you to Agnès for your help with technical issues. Thank you to Alexandre, Élise, Mathilde and Sonia.